"Bananaheart is a heart courageously exposed—the heart of a warm, brave, truthful *hapa* woman. She invites you into her loneliness, her longing and tenderness and shows you a life that is deeply lived and exquisitely observed. A powerful, moving collection."

—Joy Kogawa, *Obasan* and *Itsuka*

"Marie Hara explores how race, class, sexual politics, and the continuing influence of the colonial past shape the lives and choices of her female protagonists. "Fourth Grade Ukus," about cultural indoctrination in the public schools, is already a classic."

—Sylvia Watanabe, *Talking to the Dead*

"Marie Hara's stories are so moving, they will make you cry, and so hilarious, you will laugh aloud. These stories from the soul of immigrant Hawai'i, will reach out and find the commonality of all people. They are beautiful."

—Wakako Yamauchi, *Songs My Mother Taught Me*

"These stories are told in the variegated voices of the protagonists whom Marie Hara knows well. She is a pioneer in a literature which will grow in scope as we all—yellow, brown, red, white and black—merge in a common humanity."

—Hisaye Yamamoto DeSoto,
Seventeen Syllables and Other Stories

A Collection of Short Stories

for Mark Lofstrom ♡

BANANAHEART
& OTHER STORIES

me Ke
Aloha
Pumahana

by **MARIE HARA**

Marie Hara

BAMBOO RIDGE PRESS
1994

January 26, 1996

This is a special double issue of *Bamboo Ridge, The Hawai'i Writer's Quarterly*, issues 61 and 62 (Spring and Summer 1994), ISSN 0733-0308.

ISBN 0-910043-33-7

Cover art: "Passers-by" by Jinja Kim, 1982, etching, 7-13/16" x 4-3/4"
Title page: "Dog Album #5" by Jinja Kim, 1984, etching, 5-7/8" x 3-7/8"
Photographs of artwork: Paul Kodama
Book design: Susanne Yuu
Typesetting: Wayne Kawamoto
Printed in the United States
Published by Bamboo Ridge Press

Bamboo Ridge Press is a non-profit, tax-exempt organization formed to foster the appreciation, understanding, and creation of literary, visual, audio-visual and performing arts by and about Hawaii's people. Your tax-deductible contributions are welcomed. Bamboo Ridge Press is a member of the Council of Literary Magazines and Presses (CLMP).

This publication is supported in part by grants from the National Endowment for the Arts (NEA), a federal agency and by the State Foundation on culture and the Arts (SFCA). The SFCA is funded by appropriations from the Hawai'i State Legislature and by grants from the NEA.

NATIONAL
ENDOWMENT
FOR THE
ARTS

Library of Congress Cataloging-in-Publication Data

Hara, Marie, 1943–
Bananaheart and other stories / Marie Hara.
    p.   cm.
Contents: Honeymoon Hotel, 1895—Buddaheads, 1933—Old kimono—Watching fire—Fourth grade ukus—The gift—The curse closet—Fo' w'at stay shame—Bananaheart—A birthday card and warm wishes—You in there—Go to home.
ISBN 0-910043-33-7 : $8.00
1. Japanese American women–Hawaii–Fiction. I. Title.
II. Title: Bananaheart and other stories.
PS3558.A556B36 1994   94-29326
813' .54—dc20   CIP

BAMBOO RIDGE PRESS
P. O. BOX 61781
HONOLULU, HAWAI'I 96839-1781
(808) 599-4823

10 9 8 7 6 5 4 3 2 1   94 95 96 97 98

TABLE OF CONTENTS

*S*urely it was disappointment. A simple matter of being disappointed, certainly. That was the problem. It was clear and not unexpected by any means. Rearranging her kimono properly around her legs, she sat on a western style chair near a window which looked out across the street to a bustling park. Vendors sold food and newspapers. People in all manner of dress crossed the grass and the dirt road. She noticed Hawai'ian women in long, loose dresses. In the distance spread the bare brown and green hills which she had seen from the deck of the ship; from here the mountaintops appeared to be misty in the mid-morning sunlight.

Today as they traveled along the harbor in the open wagon, she had taken in the busyness of this town called Honolulu. Wagons, it seemed,

THE HONEYMOON HOTEL, 1895

hauled goods everywhere in an entertaining fashion. She had wanted to say, "It's not much like country living, is it?" Still she couldn't allow herself to comment so forwardly to Yamamoto-san. She kept her observations private. She missed being able to talk to Chika.

Except for Chika-san, the other women, her fellow travelers, had all been called for. Chika alone had been left to wait for her new husband. Was her fate to be preferred? Maybe Chika would have to return to Japan if she had been forgotten.

The Immigration Station was a formidable building with intricate wooden decorations all over its multi-leveled roofs and windows. It could be mistaken for a temple, except that it was hardly Japanese in feeling. After the long ship voyage every detail of life on shore took her eager interest. Life here was such a novelty, just as people promised it would be. To think of it, within a season's time she had seen both the city of Hiroshima and now, Honolulu. Remarkable. And here there were no seasons. Curious. She had thought about the persistent heat while they passed long hours in quarantine.

They had to wait endlessly. Sectioned off separately for more medical questions, then lined up all together, and finally seated in a row on a polished bench, each of the women clung to the arm of a shipboard friend. Chika and she sat tensely that way for two hours of fretful anticipation.

Her name was called. When Yamamoto-san stepped out of the group of men to claim her as his wife, Sono saw his face from the vantage of her lowered head through half-closed eyes. She had to compose herself. He looked too old! The photograph she kept in her kimono depicted a smooth-shaven young man. The Yamamoto person who stood at the desk appeared to be at least forty years old and bearded heavily. Sono felt her lower lip quiver and Chika's reassuring clutch growing tighter on her now tingling arm.

So that was how he had managed to trick the family. Certainly people had forewarned them in Hiroshima that the Hawai'i men were desperate in their desire to establish families. But Yamamoto-san was known to her uncle. Shouldn't he have prevented such an awkward match, knowing the man's true age? Sono was so obligated to Uncle, indeed, everyone was, for his support through the difficult years. But not to have guided her, when he must have known the true circumstances, his elderly friend's trickery. Yamamoto-san looked even older than her uncle when he moved about so cautiously, talking to the foreigners.

Her mind raced through scattered images, connecting her confusion with memories of her seated family, noisily discussing Sono's marriage, and her life faraway in Hawai'i. Unconcerned by the bustle of activity around the bench, she brooded in turmoil. It was Chika who timed the little push forward when the stranger turned to face her.

Sono managed, somehow, to bow and maintain a calm demeanor, while she mentally totalled his positive attributes. He did seem to be clean, prosperous and kindly. He was polite. He smiled. Truly as hard as leaving with him was saying goodbye to Chika when all the papers had been signed, all the questions answered, and all the officials signaled them outward.

For some reason the man called Miura, Seinosuke, who was Chika's husband, was not present. There must have been a delay in his traveling from another island. Without her having to ask, Yamamoto-san promised to check on Chika's situation tomorrow. She looked very unhappy, but she smiled graciously as she bid them farewell, the humiliated Chika, a lonely kimono-clad figure left waiting on the long bench. The other girls hurried off or looked away, not wanting to injure her further with their obvious pity.

When Sono walked out of the building, following Yamamoto-san to the wagon, she had no idea where they would be going. The horse-drawn vehicle, more an open air cart, carried a number of the couples past the waterfront to a three-story brick and wood building. She could not read the English name on the sign in front of the hotel. She had stayed in an inn only once before, and this could not be the same. Once in, she noticed with relief that the clerks and maids were Japanese. A tiny lobby with large chairs and sofas quickly filled up with a dozen couples and the women's large willow trunks and cloth bundles. She saw that the other girls, like herself, seemed self-conscious and subdued. Only Kono-san and her sister, Kumi-san, continued to whisper and chatter as usual. Very rudely they discussed someone whose face, it seemed, took on the appearance of "a dog when it laughs out loud." In the silence around them, smiles materialized on the faces of silent listeners. Sono did not appreciate the joke, for all she knew, they were discussing one of their own husbands.

When the manager of the hotel appeared in the main doorway, however, it became obvious that he was the one. Beaming at the company, his lip curled upward in a cockeyed manner. No one looked more like a smiling dog, Sono considered, than this slightly balding man. Suppose he had been Yamamoto-san. Sono inhaled deeply. There was a new mood of jocularity in the room; the group grew noisy.

Slowly they were being taken upstairs to their rooms. While Yamamoto-san talked with the manager at the desk, Sono gently adjusted the obi around her waist and pressed her perspiring face with a handkerchief which she had tucked away in her sleeve. A slowly growing numbness seemed to spread into her shoulders, causing her to sit up straighter and compose her features into a stern expressionlessness.

Looking surreptitiously at the other couples, she noted with fleeting envy that Tome-san was matched with a vigorous farmer. Sleepy-eyed Tome was no beauty, even as Sono assumed she herself was ordinary in looks. On ship the other women found themselves in idle agreement that Chika was the most attractive, a "born beauty." What an unlucky fate she had found in this place.

In an instant Yamamoto was leading Sono up to the little room over the street. He seemed to prance eagerly up the flights of steps.

"Leave the luggage," he counseled. "They will bring it up later."

But all of her possessions were in the *kori*. What would she have to change into, if delivery were delayed? What if someone was a thief? Frowning, Sono said nothing.

In silence they sat on the zabuton pillows set out on the grass-mat flooring. No table, no tea service, nothing but a tall chair, a lamp and a small window which drew a hazy light into the opposite end of the room, gave the space its details.

Presently her husband spoke, looking directly at her face with an appraising curiosity that embarrassed her. He asked questions about their families in Hiroshima, the crops, and the voyage across the Pacific. She answered each evenly.

"It is to be hoped, Sono-san, that you will be at home here in Hawai'i." He cleared his throat and watched her face. Yamamoto-san seemed uneasy and did not continue. He must have practiced, it was such a formal tone.

She was not able to respond and kept her head lowered. She noticed his hands were sunburnt and calloused. Did this mean he was not truly a wealthy farmer? Or was it evidence of a hard-working man?

Directing his comments to her bowed head, he stared at her thick black hair, knotted expertly at the nape of her slender neck.

"Excuse me. While we are in Honolulu, I must go for a few hours' business and will return punctually within the afternoon. Please relax here. Is there anything you would like me to purchase in the shops?"

Sono shook her head. His voice filled her ears. She would have enjoyed walking around with him, but she felt empty and wearied by his strained attempt to communicate with her.

When she was sure that he was gone, she moved to the window to look out at the activity on the ground. She could see a stream leading down from the hills to the ocean. Glittering water. How she would have enjoyed following it up and up into the misty forest. No houses were built on the mountain slopes. One could get lost in the woodsy areas. They looked quite near. And yet, of course, there was no way of knowing for sure.

Standing, she pushed the edge of the thick drapery away. From the side of the open window frame she caught a glimpse of the town. The road crossed a small bridge over flat green river water and led the way past many small shops and saloons. In the distance she saw the roof tops of stone buildings. They had passed behind that area on their way along the docks. Sono backtracked through the memory of the past few hours and the time of quarantine until she reached the weeks aboard the ship. She saw herself standing at the deck of the S.S. Intrepid, looking at the distant shore of Oahu with the tight eagerness only someone seasick too long could muster.

At her side Chika calmly observed, "So we are here after all."

Sono replied, "If only our parents could know that we have arrived safely. All their prayers. They would be gratified."

"Then for our families, sake, we must write letters to send back with the ship." Chika, so practical, comforted Sono, because she understood above all the loneliness as well as the obligation of leaving the family circle. She had been the first friend Sono had made outside of village people. In long conversations they had promised to be lifelong companions since they would be sure to see each other daily on such a small island.

So many plans had to be reconsidered. The island. The husbands. Their friendship. Everything changed as soon as they docked. What would become of Chika-san now? She wondered when she would see her friend again. For that matter, what would her own life be like with this unexpected Yamamoto?

Resigning herself to the situation, Sono tasted her disappointment without self-pity. She had learned from her earliest years that she was not going to be the child favored. That distinction went to her eldest brother. Luck was not to be Sono's domain, and untested expectations were always a mistake. She knew happiness to be a condition where simple needs were met. If there was enough food to eat, enough clothing to wear, enough fuel for warmth and enough family to gather around in enjoyment of a pleasant evening, that was enough for her lot in life. She could be content with those ingredients. She was a poor farmer's daughter who had been schooled in sacrifice. She could hear the voices of the women in her clan reminding her to be thankful that her widowed mother had one less mouth to feed.

Now here was Yamamoto-san who was happy to take care of her needs. She felt ashamed to have found him lacking. Sono knew a little about him. Everyone heard that he had been apprenticed as a carpenter. They said he was a capable man, but he loved to drink and had lost much of his parents' respect through his loose ways. City life in Hiroshima had hardened him. As soon as a friend decided to leave for California, Yamamoto took the chance of joining him to earn enough to send his family his savings. A model son, the villagers declared. He had settled in Hawai'i, and money regularly arrived in the village. Sono had been impressed by the tale. But in Hiroshima she was impressed by the first three-story building she had ever seen. She had been so impressed by the sight of the steamer that she trembled as she crossed the gangplank. No wonder her mother prayed continually for her well-being. "Is she praying?" Sono wondered. The marriage had been officially recorded. There was no turning back. "Mother, pray for me now."

Two streaks of tears formed silver pathways on the face of the young girl in the third floor window of the honeymoon hotel. She made no sound in crying and after a while turned away, her attention taken by the arrival of the willow basket the maids had carried up to the room.

The two aproned women, not much older than Sono, transferred a look which referred to the crying girl. They were sorry for her, but what could they say or do? Many of them suffered, the maids saw it all the time.

As they left, politely bowing, they called out, "Thank you, Honorable Mrs. Housewife," as might ordinarily be said, but this time they chorused their words in a childish teasing meant to bring laughter up to every listener's lips. They repeated the absurd inflection and emphasized the dignity of the word honorable with comic expressions. When they succeeded in making Sono giggle to hear their strange manner of speech, the maids thumped each other on the shoulder and disappeared down the corridor with boisterous laughter. Sono's surprise settled into restored spirits, and she began to examine the clothes and goods in her basket as if she hadn't done so dozens of times already. Each item represented the spirit of someone dear to her, and their gifts anchored her with their presence.

When Yamamoto-san returned, he knocked cautiously before he tried the door. Sono opened it carefully. To her surprise her husband handed her a large bouquet of lilies, gingers and daisies, as well as a package fashioned out of his handkerchief, tied up *furoshiki* style.

She rushed both to the window, propping the newspaper wrapped flowers against the chairback and opening the white muslin to find two pinkish guavas, a tiny mottled banana and two small Kona oranges. Sono exclaimed, and Yamamoto beamed as if to say, this is just the beginning, there will be more for you.

For the first time she spoke to him openly.

"Well, how nice of you to consider my feelings." She gazed shyly at his eyes. He coughed. Confident now that she was appreciative of his efforts and would be a responsive wife, he mumbled, "It's the least I could do to welcome you to Hawai'i." When her pale skin was flushed, Sono seemed to convey a sweet delicacy beyond the proper wifely qualities he imagined before.

Yamamoto would have enjoyed embracing her then and there as was his husbandly right. Instead, hearing a great clattering noise from the road below, he asked Sono if she had ever ridden in a mule-tram.

In confusion Sono shook her head. "A mule-tram?"

He pointed out a curious open-sided conveyance passing directly below them. It was dragged by a team of rattling collared mules. Both laughed at the same time when they caught sight of a barefooted ragamuffin sneaking a ride on the rear of the crowded tram. A small dog marked with a dark ring around one eye tried jumping up several times to join the boy on the edge of the bouncing bumper. Finally he was caught in mid-leap by his master who smiled triumphantly, showing all of his teeth to the delighted onlookers.

"Things are different here, you see."

"Yes, people can be very merry." Her head dropped again as she studied the floor.

Realizing that she had not been entirely happy waiting for him, Yamamoto decided to take Sono out for a ride to a beach area called Waikiki, past the town of Honolulu.

"Let me show you what is here. You will be amused. The ride is fast and bumpy."

The couple boarded the tram at the turn-around point adjacent to the park across the street from their hotel. Yamamoto pointed out the view sites and major buildings along the way. They sat stiffly in their best clothes, holding on to the seats and surveying all the assorted activities of the heart of the capital of the islands. Fifty-seven years later she would remind him about the miles of duck ponds and rice fields they passed before the end of the dusty road.

Through a small ironwood thicket which reminded her of certain Japanese seaside pines, they walked right next to the ever present ocean which surged and crackled at their bare feet. They carried their footwear and ate their fruit standing on the blazing beach. She became fascinated by the recurrent waves which washed fiercely against a half moon of rocky sand and stretched up to a grove of struggling coconut trees. She said, "This is not at all what I expected; it's so different."

He nodded curtly in acknowledgment without understanding her emotion. He said, "This very ocean touches our home shores. Someday we are sure to return. The gods willing, we won't be disappointed."

She turned her head and wiped away secret tears, because he was so totally convincing. He had been raised, after all, to be a chosen son. With her back to him she accepted his unwavering self confidence. She would never question his lack of worldly success in the more than half century allotted to their marriage.

From a distance the kimono-clad girl and the black-suited man seemed to be locked into a flirtatious battle of wills, a typical seaside lovers' tiff on a lazy afternoon, which resulted in his taking her hand to lead her back to the tram terminal. In truth they had merely decided to return home to their room.

All the way back, the words "we won't be disappointed" bounced through Sono's thoughts as the tram jostled them up and down from stop to stop.

Surely it was the best thing to do. Chika had accepted her fate. She could do no more. Since there was no way to be sure of anything at all at any time, Sono reminded herself, why not rest with this choice? In the matter of how to feel about things, she would remain in charge. Then it was settled; there was no problem.

The tram passed a field where a Chinese farmer guided an ox through a swampy rice paddy.

To Yamamoto-san she said, "It certainly isn't anything like the farming life we knew, is it?"

Surprised by her comment, he looked at Sono with attention to her observations. He began to tell her all the things he found unlikely or thought-provoking in the ten years since he had left home. Still in conversation when the tram pulled into the terminal, they didn't notice they had arrived home.

At dinner that evening by the doorway to the hotel's Japanese dining room, a bespectacled, portly Miura-san and his new bride Chika greeted Mr. and Mrs. Yamamoto with grateful formality. Startled, Sono grasped Chika's hand in joy.

"Chika-san!" Sono's voice tightened in escalating pleasure over the turn of events. Her friend stood surrounded by a surprising calm. As Sono studied Chika's delicate face, she thought she could see a deep relief that Miura had come to get her after all. At the table Sono decided not to say anything which might lead to further questions. They would have enough time later to discuss this day in detail, she felt certain of it.

Self-consciously dignified, Sono began to serve Yamamoto. Naturally Chika followed, and soon both women poured tea and served rice for the first time to their husbands. Acknowledging a good start and mirroring each other's pleasure, the Yamamotos and the Miuras ate their food with hearty appetites. They maintained a good-natured and respectful silence which graced their table as they ate the meal.

With sincerity the couples toasted each other, wishing themselves good luck. Others in the room looked in their direction and recognized them as fortunate.

Tomorrow they would leave for the port of Hilo and two outlying towns where they would begin the cane-growing work as family units. Tonight they would enjoy the honeymoon hotel.

A man and woman appeared at one of the third floor windows. For a moment they looked at the moonlight on the surface of the glittering river.

*T*he first time she found her way up the back stairs to the second floor bedroom, the new maid had reason to be nervous. Katie had been sent there to collect the laundry when she heard the insistent crying. A woman's voice, the sound of it distorted into a jagged sighing of exasperation came in bursts, then soft, sucking gasps. Undecipherable words rustled out from under the door of the room where she had been told the missus slept. She must dream out loud, Katie observed as she moved resolutely, bending into the hampers, gathering up clothes from the bathrooms. But she glanced around at all the rooms before hurrying downstairs to the kitchen. She had somehow expected to see Mr. Stuart's head peeking out of a doorway into her vision, although no one appeared. He was so silent anyway, she decided, he wouldn't be any help in calming such emotion.

BUDDHAHEADS, 1933

When she began to climb the carpeted stairs again, this time with a pile of stiffly ironed sheets in her arms, Katie pulled back an almost irrepressible need to let out a sound, even a snort of relief, just to test the silence. How could this have come about so quickly? Katie, so independent, so proud, getting paid for a real working day? Although they would never say so, everyone at home in Kapa'au had expected she'd return crestfallen when she figured out how hard it was to earn her own keep. A week ago she'd lived totally dependent for every meal and every cent of bus fare from Auntie Miyoko and Uncle Isamu, who had a stall at the fish market. A month ago she had waited so long staring out at the miles of cane field beyond their plantation house that she was startled when Father said that he'd decided he would let her leave for Honolulu where she might have a chance to earn her way through school. That it was true. That he allowed it. And she had been Kiyoko then because of O-Kasan's stubborn desire to keep her entirely Japanese and, of course, under her thumb. A thousand years ago, it seemed, older sister had given her two painted banners, one character signifying humility and the other, harmony, to hang up on the wall above her cot, which cluttered Uncle's dank kitchen floor but was still hers alone. And it meant she could choose whichever way she pleased to live her days.

Now she looked sharp enough in her crisp, two-piece maid's aproned uniform, her vaguely European cap squarely placed upon her head with the hair smoothed back into a neat bun. The outfit had cost Katie all of her stored up self confidence when she asked the widow, Mrs. Kameda, to lend her eight dollars and fifty cents to buy the clothing. The shoes were the big expense. Katie was all too obligated since the widow also had to beg the *haole* Mr. Stuart to give Katie, blank in experience or references, a chance to work. The monthly twelve dollars and fifty cents was big money, the bills of which Katie planned to hide in a tiny hand-stitched bag pinned into her slip, while only the loose change would be allowed out in her woven *lauhala* bag. Remembering all the while that the two daily free meals plus training counted toward making her own life, Katie couldn't afford to do any less than her best in return.

Uncle was gone at 4:30 each morning, and Auntie was ready an hour later to catch a bus downtown. Katie's first job was to clean and put away the soiled dishes after her own quick breakfast, and then to get herself to the mansion above the valley before seven o'clock when the whole staff began to ready the tables for breakfast service. So what if she had to get up at five a.m., she reasoned, that was how the day began in Kapa'au too.

Stepping out of the city bus at the foot of the massive stone wall which wrapped around the estate, Katie had been impressed. She looked up at the green lawns surrounding the big white house waiting at the end of a winding driveway under an enormous expanse of blue sky.

At first her job seemed comically easy. All she had to do was to arrange a bright array of freshly picked hibiscus blossoms. She would string these on coconut frond ribs and place several dozen colorful flowers thus skewered so that they cascaded out of sand-filled standing vases which marked the steps from the porte cochere to the awning covered front lanai. If hibiscus weren't plentiful in the bushes along the long driveway, waxy plumerias were picked with an efficient hook so that some variety of fresh flowers was formally arranged upon the white linen of the dining table.

Next Katie helped set out the breakfast dishes, depending upon the orders that had been given the night before. Curious about all the *haole* food she watched being prepared, Katie liked repeating the new names: eggs Benedict, asparagus, popovers. She felt awkward calling the widow Kameda Mitzi as did the boss lady, Mrs. Waldren, 6 feet tall, from New Jersey, who was the head housekeeper. Katie preferred not to use Mitzi's name at all over being disrespectful to Kameda-san, her benefactor. At the same time she was proud that she could say Waldren correctly, not like the others who were older and didn't do the l's and r's right, ending up with something that sounded more like Wah-len because Hawaiian, Japanese and Filipino words already filled their mouths with sound.

As she worked, Katie spent most of the first week deciding what connections people had to one another. She studied the two short, middle-aged Japanese men, who were called houseboys, and their responses to the cooks and gardeners. Each of them ruled over certain areas and took care of delineated tasks. The men, who gave away no public emotions, still behaved like the demanding elders she knew at home in the camp, who bragged to the women workers about what men would not do. They would burn the rubbish and fill the slop cans with wet garbage, but they would not wash those containers out. One of them, Hamada-san, seemed too interested by far in Kameda-san, but Katie realized it was her place not to give any sign that she noticed anything, since Mrs. Kameda was quiet on purpose about it

Once when Katie missed the early morning streetcar and arrived too late for the busiest hour, she was reprimanded severely by the boss lady. Although she was used to being scolded at home, Katie did not expect words to have sarcastic sting to them and blinked away tears with her head bent low.

"Sorry, I got late today."

Mrs. Waldren snapped back angrily, "You young Nips think you can get away with bloody murder, because all of you practice smiling up to me every day. Just because you can sit around the teapot and have your snacks out of the pantry, don't think you can take advantage of my good nature."

Katie protested before she thought out what to say. "Mrs. Waldren, we did not do anything. We following the rules." She was disturbed at the loudness of her voice as she squelched her next thought which was about the lack of choice they had in where to sit, then noticed Mitzi looking at her funny before she shut up. Oddly

Mrs. Waldren just shrugged. Katie realized that Mitzi was trying to protect her from dangerous conversations with the "no-talk" glare.

Later when they were alone, Mitzi said something Katie later picked on all the time. Mitzi asked her, "How come you talk like one *haole*? No make shame fo' me. No make big mout'. I the one brought you in, no fo'get."

Katie bowed her head silently in embarrassment. She thought about what Mitzi said while she washed the dishes or made beds. In moments of reverie she saw Mitzi's angry eyes and tight mouth and heard "like one *haole*."

In time the new maid was chosen to deliver Mrs. Stuart's breakfast to her room at exactly nine o'clock each morning. Dull silver satin drapes, which reached up to the rounded arches of the windows, were securely closed.

Not a sound entered the room with the girl's arrival. Weeks later during a quiet moment Katie peeked out from a small balcony just to see what the gardens looked like below.

Always nestled heavily in sleep, Mrs. Stuart wrapped in linen sheets, was the central point of the pale greys and finely graded white stripes within the shrouded room. A bowl of gardenias spread a cool scent through the air. Katie tiptoed in and pulled the cord to a porcelain lamp, which centered its pearly light on the tray of food she left on the bedside table. As she tiptoed out again, she exhaled relief. The sleeping form silhouetted under shimmering covers did not stir at all.

"She's going to wake up when the weather comes hot?" Katie asked Mitzi.

"No. She would never wake up until the afternoon."

"But why do we serve her food so early?"

"The husband say so. You better remember *haole* house you don't ask why."

As she dusted a silver frame that enclosed a photograph of the Stuarts raising their glasses in a toast, Katie wondered about them.

Mr. Stuart, she saw every day as he ate his two poached eggs and read his newspaper without a word to anyone. When she thought once that he was speaking to her, it was instead the sound of his blowing his nose. He appeared to be very large, balding, and the most preoccupied human being she had ever observed. He often ignored guests who had stayed the night. Mr. Stuart had a way of riveting her attention without ever looking at her. He merely pointed at his cup, and Katie felt commanded to quietly refill it.

One day Mrs. Stuart was up at nine. Wide-eyed, she looked carefully at Katie when she entered with the tray.

"Put it here by the mirror."

Thin as a venetian blind's slat, Mrs. Stuart turned out to have inordinately pale skin and intense features. The fine remnants of eye liner and mascara circled her deep eyes in black. She looked as weary and enervated as an invalid who struggled greatly just to be able to be heard.

The young girl studied her face, unsure what to say.

"You're okay, ma'am?" Katie did not realize that this woman did not want to be appraised. Mrs. Stuart's anger was a puzzle.

"Don't be impertinent, missy. Get me a towel from the bathroom." She pointed to a door. "Hurry."

Katie placed it carefully on the seated woman's lap.

"You can go. And I don't need any more help. Tell Waldren that."

Katie left as quietly as she could, remembering the modulated elegance in the missus's voice, which made her skin creep. She resolved to stay away from the kitchen to avoid serving Mrs.

Stuart her breakfast again. The surprise the next day was that Mrs. Stuart requested her presence.

Hearing an unmistakable retching, Katie stopped short at the door before she knocked. Mrs. Stuart wiped her mouth and waited without expression when Katie entered. Only a sour smell from sweat that rolled down the edges of Mrs. Stuart's face gave a sign of her previous vomiting. She gestured to the maid to sit down in the armchair. A white silk kimono, worn like a robe, was wrapped around her thin frame. Her jewelry from the night before had been left on or forgotten. A diamond-studded bangle bracelet caught the lamplight as she carefully tapped the ashes from her cigarette into the silver wire crosshatches which formed a grating over an ornate filigreed ashtray.

"Now tell me how old you really are. I can never tell looking at you girls."

"I'm seventeen, no, eighteen, now." Katie shook her head at her own desire to speak in proper English. If she felt surprised at the questioning, her curiosity about the woman before her kept her involved in the process of delivering answers.

Mrs. Stuart couldn't stop staring at Katie. She seemed curious although nervous about every detail of her maid's life: what she liked to eat, what colors, what movies, what popular songs, what movie stars Katie liked. Katie answered everything pleasantly. She volunteered some information, confiding that she planned to get a bob and a permanent wave when she had enough money set aside. Mrs. Stuart asked nothing about her family or where she was from. Katie noticed that she didn't use her name at all.

The chatter stopped when she handed Katie an initialed silver brush and directed her with a motion to brush her shoulder-length brown hair. It was thin and fine, unlike the thick hair of her sisters, which Katie was used to working into plaits and coils. Katie gave all her energy to doing the missus's hair to a shine. The brushing appeared to relax her. After a while Mrs. Stuart said, "You can go now. Take the tray with you. And don't forget that." She pointed at the heap of stained towels on the floor. Katie silently did as she was told, but wondered if she should say goodbye.

She said nothing as she left.

The next day it was the same. Even the questions were more of the same. But Mrs. Stuart asked a disturbing thing with no possible answer.

"Why do you stare at me? Why do you watch me all the time?"

For no reason Mrs. Stuart opened the drawer to her bedside stand and let Katie see a small marble sculpture. It was the head of a pretty girl who looked wide eyed and open mouthed. Because the eyes were open, she looked blind, but Katie was also curious as she tried to understand what Mrs. Stuart repeated so softly. "My baby, my little girl." She said it twice.

Mrs. Stuart seemed to be talking more to herself than to Katie.

Katie grew increasingly uncomfortable at the thought of returning daily for more emotional talking, even if she didn't have to say anything. Slowly, Katie puzzled over Mrs. Stuart's being kind to her whenever she thought about it. Feeling somewhat embarrassed by the sentiments, she nursed something else the older woman had said, "Someday, you could be like a daughter to me. I could teach you everything you need to know and make it worth your while. But first you will have to do what I ask you to." Katie almost asked what that would be but remembered Mitzi's advice to keep silent with *haoles*. Since Katie figured she was already doing exactly what was required, she had smiled blankly, considering mothering someone wasn't what the missus would ever really do, and left without comment.

The next morning Mrs. Waldren turned things around by voicing her suspicion that Katie was "trying to play favorites with Mrs. Stuart." In her anger she sent Mitzi upstairs with the tray. She missed the great relief which traveled through Katie's face. Worried earlier that she would be fired, Katie found dusting or dishwashing was not the annoyance that Mrs. Waldren supposed it would be to her. She was also given the extra chore of washing only the fine silk underwear and certain lace blouses, nightgowns and hose that Mrs. Stuart wore. Waldren scowled and said she wasn't satisfied with the way they had been ironed. She directed Katie to press and fold them in "the French way, not like a common Chinese laundry. Orientals have no understanding of how to do things correctly."

Katie swallowed her words of protest as useless. Mitzi shrugged her shoulders when she heard the demand. In explanation to Katie, Mitzi said, "Make 'um any kine. Starch 'em hard if get cotton part and iron wet fo' da silk kine. Jes' stiff, nuff." So Katie meticulously washed and ironed the delicate pieces until they were barely dry and relished the sight of luxurious lace, elaborate patterns and hidden fastenings that took her away almost pleasantly from certain trouble, whatever it might be.

First enjoying the work with cool water, Katie began to worry that she spent too much time in the laundry shack in a reverie of wearing elegant clothing and even more beautiful underwear, unknown to anyone she talked to at gala, flower-filled parties. At the real ones, she knew there was nothing at all she had to do but serve and clean up. It didn't matter what she wore, even her own homemade rice bag cotton pants, because she was invisible as a servant. As Katie hung up the silk underwear, she felt for a moment that she was being watched by someone and looked around. There was no one. But she moved back into the outdoor shed, out of the bright light. Standing near the wash trough, she looked cautiously at the damp cement floor. She had heard a clicking, shuffling noise and watched the last part of a good-sized centipede scurrying away into the wood rot.

Imaginary parties entertained her, but the best feeling was to be left alone. Then she was safe. She wasn't so much afraid as annoyed by the strange *haole* men who came to the Stuarts' parties and who looked at her with either condescension, seeing past her as if they looked at the furniture, or with an eagerness to cage her attention one way or another, which they alone initiated with prodding and insinuating questions asked on the sly.

"So, you work here, do you now?"

"Hot enough for you, tonight? Must've come from one of the out-islands, right? Which one?"

They never asked her name or spoke to her in the tone with which they carried on other social conversations. Their loud, joking bluster was gone when they looked at her plain face and spoke softly, hurriedly, while they waited impatiently for her murmured "Yes, sir" or occasional "No, sir" as she walked away backwards. Working at a *haole* house was harder than she thought when she had to decide what was expected of her from contradictory people. If she were asked for a drink or told directly to take a message, she felt she was doing the work she had been hired to do. To talk on a personal level was not her work. The men who arrived at the house were not really interested in her, anyway. She overheard one admonish another not to "talk in front of Japs." When they directed a comment to her, she considered them to be merely practicing before they would talk to the arriving company or the missus who took her good time about appearing at her own parties.

Few women were ever invited, and Mrs. Stuart preferred to see her guests slightly drunk before she began to drink with them.

Unpredictably Mr. Stuart sometimes returned after a party was over. Katie didn't ever want to be caught talking with him or one of the guests, especially as the drinking went on and Waldren made her periodic checks.

All her life Katie had heard that "*haole* men only afta one t'ing." In the kitchen, Katie overheard Hamada-san saying something familiar about it to a Filipino carpenter, something that ended in "da *haole* like taste *daikon*, 'as why dey go fo' Japanee girl." Even an overly friendly missionary who appeared at the Stuarts' very early for a party couldn't get her to say more than "No, sir." In a confidential tone as he waited for the rest of the guests, he told her about his plans to go to China and set up churches there. He added something heartfelt about Christ's martyrdom and turned to the maid for a response. She avoided his eyes and held out a tray of hors d'oeuvres.

Katie was not going to be forced into a conversation with anyone so stupid as to expect her to break the rules of her role as a competent maid. She couldn't afford to be angry, but she held her ground. He spoke directly to her, his intelligent eyes eager for a conversation.

"So . . . miss, now tell me, what do you think of my trip?"

She shrugged her shoulders, froze her no-expression mien and backed off. Let him think her stupid. Let him think whatever he wanted.

She remembered Reverend Webb at home. He would be content if you nodded your head. You didn't have to talk. If you did, he tsked at your pidgin English and corrected you so that you had to repeat yourself after him. Then everyone else made fun of your stupidity.

"Tryin' to act like one *haole*. Hah! *Haolified*."

She would never let such a thing be said about her. She squirmed at the thought.

Moving herself with purpose into the staircase dominated reception room, she surveyed the furniture she had dusted earlier. Nothing in the downstairs parlors was without its purpose. A grand piano gleamed in readiness for whatever gaiety might transpire. It caught the light of the declining sun, while the potted ferns seemed thicker and more luxuriant than rows of shrubs in dewy green that were the bushes framing the large yard outside.

Rank and status to a high degree showed in every object that decorated the rooms. A photo in a silver frame caught Mrs. Stuart in her fragile youth looking petulant and tired. A cabinet of liquor, a cut glass decanter, a crystal-handled letter opener were clearly his. There wasn't an object that was distinctly marked as the missus's choice in all the uncluttered rooms, although she had probably chosen most of the furnishings.

A finger to the high polish on a *koa* table, Katie heard someone playing the piano. The young man, his hair parted precisely in the middle of his forehead, sat playing the keys. His energy did not flag for several hours although the guests had moved out onto the other terraces and the individual gardens just before sunset. He gave her a brilliant smile. Katie was thrilled to listen to the popular melodies and concert pieces, but afraid to be caught in the living room with the guest. She listened from the pantry, pretending to be at work on the tray of glasses she served.

During that party, in the first conversation she had with Mrs. Stuart outside of the bedroom, Mrs. Stuart mistook Katie for Mitzi. Although they did not resemble each other in any way since they were shaped, aged and dressed differently, their Japanese faces—said Mitzi, laughing about the error later—must have "t'row her off, plus she all drunk."

Mrs. Stuart had caught Katie's eye first, by waving her glass.

"Mitzi," her high voice the first clue, "now do run and bring me another. Good girl."

Mrs. Stuart was showing her guests—several most animated and fluttery women were included—some antique celadon pieces in cases, and she grew impatient. When Katie returned, Mrs. Stuart took the drink and continued to describe the items of what she called "Stuart's booty." With a sweeping gesture her hand included the entire room while her face registered no special emotion. The intense monologue continued as the group moved on. Worried that Mrs. Stuart would suddenly spill her glass, Katie was immediately there when she did. On her hands and knees as she wiped up the glass and liquor, Katie heard the women work in concert to soothe the flustered Mrs. Stuart. They sounded like pigeons cooing and twittering. A few moments later, Katie watched them leave the room, glad to be able to think quietly as she waited.

The illusion of having this time to herself was emphasized by the sound of the steady rain outdoors, the constant dripping turning the air progressively colder. Her skin became clammy at the thought of walking in that shiny landscape where everything shimmered. If she got soaked, her uniform would have to be washed an extra time. She considered without pleasure the large park she had to cross in order to get to the main road. The walk across the wet grass caused her to become melancholy and remember her own home and her family. She decided there would be no point in getting caught again in the familiar pain. She would keep herself busy. Katie watched the other guests scurry up toward the house. Just as they returned, the rain stopped over the wet gardens which ran up to the hills.

Using an *auwai* and part of a running stream, someone, probably Mr. Stuart, had created a complicated landscape. To one side the two Filipino gardeners had been shown how to translate the design of a formal English garden into reality on a wet tropical island. It was a maze of thick hedging which led to a central point, a compact well encircled by orderly rows of flowers. Here delicate roses and extra large asters, which bowed to the ground because their heavy heads burdened their stalks, were cultivated at great expense by the gardening crew.

On the other side of the water, against the green, corrugated cliffs, a vigorous tropical jungle spread out, unlike an actual wilderness in that so many textures and multiple colors emerged to the eye of the visitor who followed the defined but meandering path.

During Katie's walk into that side of the Stuart property, she noticed for the first time the statues set up in the shrubbery. The ancient forms, some Buddhas, others dancing figures, appeared one after another, much like the riotous plant life. She wondered where they came from; India, Afghanistan, China, Japan, Korea, Burma, and Siam were the countries named on brass plaques fixed to their pedestals, although she couldn't see why they were taken from those places. Each element was not only unusual but also shocking, because it was one more richness in an already texture crowded backdrop. Worse, each piece looked abandoned.

Toward the end of the walk the larger Buddha and deity heads, bodiless and mostly the same size, each atop its concrete pedestal, were lined up one after another, a multitude of images lapped by vines and leaves. She could hear the sound of the stream flowing nearby, beyond the path.

As she moved rapidly past each of the heads, Katie grew uneasy. She was aware that most had been taken from decapitated bodies and spirited away from their proper settings. The visionless eyes of the stone heads, their bland cheeks and some jeweled necks disturbed her without her knowing why. The place didn't feel good. The unfairness of the collection of heads displayed casually in the garden struck her.

Although they were not the familiar gilt temple figures she had seen hundreds of times in her life when she attended Buddhist services, the resemblance to what she knew so well caused her to worry. For a moment she imagined another image: a row of headless crucifixes lined up in the tropical garden. Erasing it nervously, she moved on, hurrying herself. *Not lucky to think l'dat, . . . no, gotta say, 'like that, that way'*," she corrected herself, repeating the phrase like a charm. Superstition unnerved her, causing her to get thoroughly rattled when a peacock wandered onto the path.

The bird spread out its fan of feathers directly in front of Katie and squawked fiercely, it's metallic eye on her. For once Katie could see no beauty in such a chance gift of the display, but felt instead a shiver of alarm from the bird's high-pitched screeching. Katie read it as a warning.

She whirled backwards to see if a retreat would be quicker and panicked when she noticed how dark the path behind her had become. The peacock moved in jerky struts back into the under-growth as Katie ran toward the main house.

She stared at an unfamiliar thicket of cascading vines near a pandanus tree that crowded a section of the path. Or had she taken a wrong turn? The thorny branches had grown fierce in the winter rains and covered the meandering trail. She would have to either break the green vines and touch the sharply spiked leaves or else maneuver around them without getting scratched. Since she wasn't eager to do either, she pivoted to retrace her steps.

"Aaah . . . ." She stopped breathing when she saw who had been following her. It was Mr. Stuart standing halfway down the trail, not quick enough to duck behind one of the bushes. He had unbuttoned his trousers. His flaccid penis slowly staggered into erection. Mr. Stuart turned away, but not before he knew she had seen what he wanted her to. Recognizing her alarm, he gave Katie a leering smile, one with cadaverous teeth and a sardonic challenge in it. His head tilting in her direction, he pointed back to the house. Then he walked away casually as if he had meant to all along. She watched his large frame move away from her with relief.

Her confusion and defensiveness made her short of breath. She was also angry, which upset her further. She wondered if he would tell Waldren, then realized he had left the house in secret also. She told herself to stay far away from him at all times. Should she ask Mitzi for advice? Katie felt like crying, then steadied her feelings, shaking her body and running her hands down in cleaning movements to shake curses off as she had learned to at home. Long strokes down her front, her arms and the back of her head restored her balance. She began to run toward the house. Remembering herself as she reached the lawn, she walked cautiously, exposed now and worried as she checked the view behind her across the grass.

When the kitchen door closed, she breathed out a mocking laugh to herself, glad that no one had spotted her. She wanted to be considered a mature working woman, not a flighty girl. She would erase any thought about Mr. Stuart, "*no sense worry fo' notting.*" After all, he hadn't grabbed her. And she knew now what to expect. Anchoring herself behind a work table, she hurriedly began to polish the pieces of silverware in the heap set out for the next evening's party. She arranged her small, all-purpose smile carefully to hide anything that might show the fear she folded away.

Mrs. Waldren came to the kitchen doorway.

"You're dismissed for the evening. That means you can leave early. And Katie, you aren't to hang around the house."

Instead of her usual elation over extra time for herself, Katie moved out very slowly. She should have been very happy since Hamada-san had left her a paper bag of rough textured red lychees and glistening blue-green mangos which she would have to leave until she caught a ride with him and Mitzi on another day. She could hear the brown doves calling low trills to each other as they courted. There was a large flock of them on the ground, moving in and out of the shade under the banyan tree. They would stay there into the early evening while the sky deepened into a streaked red.

She had never wondered until now. Where did they go? Were they tucked in between the leaves of all the bushes and trees? How did they manage to live on their own? To eat? Were they huddled together in the eaves of the big house to stay out of the rain?

The birds, like Mrs. Stuart, were not her *kuleana*, not her obligation in any way beyond the job. She had no personal relationship with them, and they did not care about her either.

As she took the steps from the kitchen, Katie thought she heard mynahs squawking. She looked up at the electric lines stretching from the house to the nearest pole and dismissed the thought. Her spine prickled.

"No. Not birds."

As she walked, she thought she heard her name whispered.

"Kay-tee."

She remembered the peacock's bleating shriek.

When she turned to look at the house, she saw the woman's head at an open second story window.

Mrs. Stuart. She had been watching. She did know her name. Maybe Mrs. Stuart had seen her husband in the garden following after her. Mrs. Stuart was mouthing words. Katie couldn't hear the sounds, but what she meant was clear. Come up, said her silent mouth.

The pale head in the window was expressionless except for a smile or a grimace, it was hard to tell which. The eyes were blank and unfocused. A necklace around its neck glittered sharply as a flash of the jewelry picked up a glint of light.

Katie's eyes flickered in alarm. No, Mrs. Stuart couldn't have seen down into the rear garden. *Something else.* The thought arrived with a plain certainty.

"Some kinda trouble. She going tell me one lie. I no' like hea' dat kine."

Katie thought of the headless statues and pictured Mrs. Stuart, her mouth a wailing O, her jeweled neck, as if her head were on a pedestal in the garden.

Katie hesitated for a minute, grown used to taking orders from the people in this household, believing that she understood what they wanted. Katie turned around, her face now empty of expression, the emotion guarded. She would take care of it, her way. By finding another job so that she wouldn't become like Mitzi, the Stuarts' girl. By saying nothing at all, staring past the mister if she ever had to look at him. By revealing nothing, not any word of recrimination. By calming the missus and then going home alone, silent with the secrets held tightly for all the long years after, past the war, past statehood, long past the time the big *haole* houses were gone. By remembering them.

*F*rom the moment she saw it folded neatly on the top of the pile of old clothing, she was sure it would look good on her.

"One of a kind, a perfect find."

The color was right, a sophisticated black crepe. The design was just what she hoped for, "Japanese-y" and clearly ethnic, plus the incredible price. It was second hand, of course, but the jagged scrap of masking tape stuck on to it read three dollars. Three dollars. For something antique and classy. You couldn't go wrong.

People she knew or had heard about, women her age, were using old kimonos in intriguing ways, pleating them for sophisticated skirts and cutting them up for fashionable blouses and vests. If they couldn't sew, they found dressmakers. And why not? Old material turns worthless forgotten in camphor chests or left in closets as termite food. And the patterns . . . you couldn't find that kind of design on bolts anymore . . . they had become  priceless. Her own creative idea was simple: this one would be the perfect robe over a silky, black nightgown. No matter whose it had once been, it was destined to be part of her own wardrobe now, finally appreciated for its true worth, its one-of-a-kind lining, its fashion statement, subtle, but bold.

She held it up to the two elderly Japanese women who were tending their booth. The crowd at the Shinshu Mission Bazaar milled through displays of housewares and knickknacks. Most people stepped right past the rack of dark "Baba-san" dresses and assorted heaps of cast-off garments.

OLD KIMONO

The annual fair attracted a varied clump of people to the temple on a winding street off the heart of downtown Honolulu. Shoppers moved through tents and stalls. Some waited for the next batch of homemade sushi while a wave of smoke from the huli-huli chicken barbecue next door forced the bystanders to move aside or cover their watering eyes. The temple, a vestige of the 1920s, was bright pink, concrete East Indian style architecture. Easy to spot but hard to figure how it could have been built by Japanese Americans in Hawai'i, the temple now rarely attracted the young, except at Bon Dance time or the fair. So her first reaction whenever she visited was to open her eyes to take it all in once again. Here, lay evidence of good luck, the very blessing she remembered a priest telling her grandmother she would receive for faithfully visiting the memorials to the dead.

The two old ladies saw her growing interest. As the women examined the garment, they noted her enthusiasm by exchanging questioning looks. She ran her hands over the elaborate design one more time. Her action was closely watched by the hunchbacked old lady whose neck was frozen in a perpetual bow.

""Young girlu-san." She got her attention.

"Saah . . . befo' time . . . you know Watanabe-san? Yuriko? The family wen' donate all her clothes after the one-year service." This from the elderly woman with mottled age spots all over her face and arms.

With annoyance at the unasked-for information, the young woman shook her head. "Maybe my grandma might have, but I nevah come to temple nowadays."

"You know how fo' wear this kind?"

"Sure, but I might change it and maybe cut it all up, too. I don't wanna wear dis kine old-fashion stuff. In Hawai'i, too hot."

As the other one stared, the young woman pressed three bills into the hand of the silent old lady and quickly packed the neat kimono—now a precisely folded rectangle—into her designer-label satchel. Without a word the hunched one handed her a stained, cotton obi, more a child's sash than a proper waist piece. She noted also that neither of the two women thanked her, even as they carefully watched her walk away.

Hypocrites. They think they know how to do things right . . . but it's always their way or no way. Typical! In her mind's eye she saw a long line of Japanese mothers, aunties and other older women lecturing young girls relentlessly about how to do things correctly, what they meant was *perfectly.* Even creasing a line in paper had to be done just so, with the edge of a fingernail. Crazy women. She would never do it their way. Leaving them far behind in her thoughts, she freed the kimono from any further association with such negative types.

No matter what anyone might say—and it would be some old lady for sure—she wouldn't tell where she bought it. This black silk kimono held so many possibilities. Even the glossy satin collar lining was quite elegant in a crisp way; there wasn't a single stain or moth hole. Not a whiff of camphor clung to the garment. Under her stroking touch, as she felt it in her handbag on the bus ride home, the kimono took on the form of a dozen different outfits, all hers.

The frame house on Pua Lane was surrounded by helter-skelter plantings. The varicolored ornamental growth winding along a flourishing garden of rows of green onion and lettuce ruffled out all around the neatly painted building. Vaguely similar to the other homes which formed a short row along the street, the brown cottage could have been a variant of the standard, now vanished plantation house. Littered with assorted slippers and shoes, the front porch where she dashed off her sandals stopped her motion for only the briefest moment.

She stood fixed in front of a full-length mirror. She sighed in satisfaction at the blackness of the top half of the kimono held next to her skin. The mirror gave proof that her choice, the sophisticated black and exquisite design work were exactly right for her. She would look bold and new: Asian, not oriental. Sexy, not cute. The silky fabric confirmed her choice.

Once she turned the garment inside out to satisfy herself, she saw how painstakingly it had been made. Every seam was hidden by a double fold; every visible stitch, each identical to the eye, had been put in with stunning regularity since they were not machine made. Delighted, she said aloud, "My precision kimono!" held it to her chest, then frowned when she rechecked the sewing. She began to turn the kimono rapidly, then frantically. Where would the knots go? They had to be there or the whole thing would have fallen apart. All the finely matched rectangular pieces would break away. She chewed the logic of no anchor knots. Certainly they must be subtly hidden under the precise seams, of course.

At this comforting thought, she caught a glimpse of her mom's arrangement of what she called boy flawahs, anthuriums, in a blue vase placed on a bureau behind her. The red and pink flowers with their knobby pistils and sturdy stems, seemed—the only word she could call up to fit—crude. Not only were they ordinary and not placed in any particular order, they were also in no way fragile or aesthetic. They were so . . . local. Only hours away from the yard with its motley vegetation, the anthuriums shone out in their robust colors. They had been inserted into the vase for no particular reason, one more thing that her mother did by habit, not design.

By contrast the pattern of cranes and tortoises in a bamboo forest with a garden lantern, wisteria vines and chrysanthemums worked into a delicate but elaborate balance at the bottom of the kimono, spoke of art. Here lay the world where every fine line of distinguishing detail existed to make a difference. And then the crest needed some accounting for as well. On either breast, at the center back line and at two places below the shoulders, a tiny *mon* had been meticulously embroidered in white-gold thread. Whoever sewed it must have been a red hot seamstress, maybe a professional who had studied hard and aimed for perfection. She couldn't make out what the symbol meant but recognized a flower and the shape of a bird in the quarter of an inch allotted. The beak was sharply delineated.

Considering the imagery as she ran her hand wistfully over the garment now carefully spread out over the bed, she decided wearing it would make her not only look fashionably Japanese but also like someone who was used to wearing one. The only problem was that she'd have to learn all the finer points: what kind of under kimono and undergarments to wear, how to fix her hair just so, how to get her feet to walk together right and maybe even more. The kimono looked like the first step on a tiresome road of tasks to learn.

So she would use it as a simple robe. It looked like something from a fashion magazine. She was flexible. Easy elegance, that was just what she wanted from the moment she saw it. How would it look with a wide open neck and a flowing, loose sash?

When she saw herself in it for the first time, she felt a curious prickle run down her neck. It fit perfectly. That word again. She used the lightweight sash to tie herself in tightly. She wouldn't have to worry about a new hem, since it had been sewn precisely into an expert roll of one-fourth inch at the bottom edge. As she gazed at herself in the long mirror, she saw a young woman who, when she swept her full head of hair upward to form a ponytail, then a tight bun, was transformed into someone very much like a traditional Japanese woman, suddenly more demurely feminine than she had ever looked. Her form was elegantly contained in the decorated kimono column.

Oddly, she had a hard time meeting her own eyes in the mirror. She had to first look up and break out of the posture of her head bowed toward the kimono's border and the floor. She suppressed an impulse to move toward the kitchen to prepare a kettle of green tea.

Mother would bust laughing.

She chuckled, too, to think of the necessity to trot absurdly in this tight garment. Hilarious. She positioned her feet slightly inward so that the right pigeon-toed stance greeted her eyes when she admired herself again.

The blackness of the silk crepe glistened under the overhead light. To be so encased began to feel seductive. She could imagine being totally in control of an audience of observers who followed every movement she made . . . as if she were about to demonstrate an important cultural activity, explaining the reasons why people should choose this way, the proper one. Not that way, and why it looked so much more graceful, much better in the way that she had presented the action. What was the action? Just the way, actually the exquisite style with which she lifted her forearm and readied her own now elegant, elongated hand in a formal gesture of pointing to her slender form in the mirror. Her hand looked much longer, the nails subtly and perfectly shaped.

"Simple—absolutely simple—but correct, in fact, perfect." The last word came out in a pronouncement of satisfaction, although whispered.

She gazed at her image in the mirror. The Japanese-looking woman in disarray who returned the glance from the glass was vaguely familiar. With a realignment of her body posture, she saw what she would look like were she more attentive to details. The line of her back now had some starch to it, and her face grew masklike as if dreaming deeply. Erasing her individual expression, she had traded it for something more adequately female. Her eyes looked down.

One hand at her side, she fingered the cranes and tortoises and felt at home, no longer lost somewhere where the symbols meant nothing.

The figure in the sophisticated black kimono stared back at her without curiosity. With every tiny motion, her own breathing became part of a larger rhythm, something as ancient as the pattern on the cloth. She began to think about the Japan she had never seen, *tatami* mats and courtyards, wet garden stones and bustling street fronts, a Japan which she would never see, since it was all gone anyway. The romance of that charming past, replete with beckoning lanterns grew into colorful sweetmeats for her imagination. Lost in long, pleasant moments of a dream world layered with images from the Japanese movies she had gone to see with her grandma, her body began to fit the old kimono.

Her loyalty would never waver; she would serve her lord courageously. Her training would not let her do anything else. Her face would betray no emotion. Her feelings would be replaced by her purpose. She would learn what the great Lord Buddha taught about equanimity. Only her eyes would express how she regarded the universe: matter-of-factly, steadfastly seeing beauty in nature, in all the simple things, in respectfully acknowledging even bothersome people. She would lead by actions, not words.

The hour went by, the minutes unnoticed as she receded into deep thoughts about her role as a woman who appreciated the aesthetic above all. Beauty and pride, discipline and high endeavor ruled her very being.

When she let down her long hair in a straight mass against the back of the kimono, the black tresses looked like a silky waterfall with the light of the day outside picking up shiny glints in the flowing strands which moved together as one.

She pivoted slowly on one foot just to see if she could move correctly. Her hand daintily tucked back into her sleeve, she minced in tiny steps as if in time to a persistent koto melody. Back and forth, back and forth, she moved. Her face was determined as she disallowed herself a smile at the pleasing image of herself as a dancer, while she hid her hands within the kimono's delicate openings so that she looked more childlike and helpless. She cocked her head just so. No teeth, no fingernails, nothing sharp or jarring, broke her peaceful demeanor or the smooth lines of her softness dancing.

In the mirror someone diminutive and guileless reflected light. Music in her head, ringing with the rollicking cadences of koto and samisen, rushed her into electric motion, back and forth, back and forth, until she collapsed on the bed, giggling at the spectacle.

She caught her breath when she looked backwards at the mirror. The woman in the black kimono was still dancing as if the music had increased its frantic rhythm. Back and forth, back and forth: her motions were hypnotic.

Lifting her face, the dancer, caught in the instance of clapping her hands, froze at the sight of the woman staring at her from the bed.

Both gasped, the young woman and the reflection in the mirror, when the bedroom door opened.

Her mother peered in from the darkened hallway.

"Oh. You. I thought I heard music. W'at did you put on? Hmmm . . . nice. But you have it on backwards. You wen' fo'get! Always wrap da kimono left over right or else you gonna look like one dead man. Fo' real! Anybody who know anyt'ing—all da people who see dat—dey gonna laugh at you."

She was ready to explain more and give examples from her experience.

Her daughter's face must have discouraged her, because she departed without waiting for a response.

The used kimono was left in a heap on the bed.

*U*ntil the right time came for me to meet my father, I would be patient. Mama made plans all the time. She had figured out what to do. Soon after we settled into a small rental house, we walked over to Lincoln School, a gracious stone building with many trees. None of the students there had to do any manual labor. They used the newest books. They were always featured in newspaper articles and photos that she pointed out to me. Mama had heard that the best Lincoln graduates were sometimes accepted into the private high schools, which was how they "got ahead."

Once in the office I saw that all the teachers were *haole,* and it was a good thing I wore the socks and new shoes Mama had adjusted. I sat with each foot in her lap and great impatience to get accepted. Several teachers watched me watching the other kids playing on the immaculate playground equipment. This part was called The Observa-

FOURTH GRADE UKUS

tion. Once outdoors I took my time taking off my shoes and socks to keep them good for the next wearing. I kept munching softly on a strand of hair that hung comfortably near my mouth. Mama sat on a bench away from the other chatting mothers. She had one bare foot out of her slipper and rested it on top of the other foot still in its slipper. They, too, were new and hurt her. She looked tired. She was still waiting to hear about a better job than being a cook in a dormitory. I could see thoughts which made her cranky cross her face.

By the time we were back in the office for the part called The Interview, which was really a test to see if I could speak perfect Standard English, I knew something was funny. I could smell it.

The woman tester was young and Japanese and smiley. I relaxed, thought for sure I wouldn't have to act "put on" with her. But she kept after me to say the printed words on the picture cards that she, now unsmiling, held before my eyes.

"Da bolocano," I repeated politely at the cone-shaped mountain where a spiral of smoke signaled into the crayon-shaded air. She must have drawn it.

She shook her head. "Again."

"Da BO-LO-CA-NO," I repeated loudly. Maybe like O-Jiji with the stink ear on his left side, she couldn't hear. "We wen' go 'n see da bolocano," I explained confidentially to her. And what a big flat *puka* it was, I thought, ready to tell her the picture made a clear mistake.

"It's the vol-cano," she enunciated clearly, forcing me to watch her mouth move aggressively. She continued with downcast eyes. "'We went to see the vol-cano.' You can go and wait outside, okay?"

Outside I wondered why—if she had seen it for real—she drew it all wrong.

Mama shrugged it off as we trudged home.

"Neva' mind. Get too many stuck shet ladies ova dea. People no need act, Lei. You wait. You gon' get one good education, not like me."

That was how I ended up at Ka'ahumanu School which was non-English Standard. Its front yard sported massive flower beds of glowing red and yellow canna lilies arranged in neat rows, which were weeded and watered daily by the students. Teachers at Ka'ahumanu were large in size, often Hawaiian or Portuguese with only an occasional wiry Chinese or Japanese lady in sight. There was a surprise *haole* teacher who came in to teach art and hug kids. Many teachers wore bright hibiscus blooms stuck into their pugs of upswept hair. They didn't hold back on any emotions as they swept through the main yard like part of a tide of orderliness, lining up their wriggly children into classes. They cuffed the bad and patted the heads of the obedient as they counted us. They were magnetic forces with commanding voices, backbones at full attention and bright flowers perched like flags on the tops of their heads. When we stood in formation, the first ritual of the morning, rumors of all kinds went through our lines. I learned right away that on special holidays the cafeteria might even serve *laulau* and *poi* which we would help to prepare. Now that was worth waiting for.

I had resolved that in Honolulu I would have friends "fo' real." To this goal I studied the children at play and kept a silent watch before venturing in. When I forgot this logic and opened my mouth, it almost cost me my appetite to get educated. Because I occupied a fantasy world of vividly drawn characters from books and people I had made up for the lonely times in Kohala, I could go "off on a toot" and momentarily forget the real ones in front of me. I had gotten used to amusing myself in that way even while other kids swirled in activity around me.

I was in a dreamy mood when I first ran into Mrs. Vincente, who was to be my teacher. As a human being she was an impressive creation, since her bulk was unsettling and her head quite small. As she waddle-walked toward me, I made a fatal error. I mistook her for an illustration in a library book I had grown fond of in Kohala. She was a dead ringer for the character I thought I was seeing right before my nose. And why not? The first day of school was supposed to be the beginning of new and exciting things in my life. Everything so far had been surprising.

Therefore, I squealed out loud in pleasure, "Oh, Mrs. Piggy-Winkle!" at the sight of the pink-fleshed mountain topped by a salad plate-sized orange hibiscus. Did I truly think she would be equally delighted to see me? Mrs. Vincente, as I learned later, would never forget me. At the moment of our meeting, she grabbed me by the back of my neck and shook me fiercely until I blubbered.

Teachers came running; students formed a mob around our frantic struggling, and the school principal, Mrs. Kealoha-Henry, saved me.

As I stood sobbing in shivers from the wild shaking, Mrs. Vincente lectured me and the others on good manners. I shook my head in a no-no-no when she asked in an emotional voice, "Do you understand now?" It took all of Mrs. Kealoha-Henry's counsel to keep Mrs. Vincente away from me.

Grabbing the opportunity, I ran all the way back home where long after she came home from work, Mama found me hiding out in the laundry shed. I didn't return to school for several days after that. But my mother's continual nagging, bribery and my own plain boredom finally wore me down. I vowed not to talk at school, in the name of personal safety. And I would forget imagination.

When I returned, I learned another lesson, although this one, also, started out in confusion. Back at Ka'ahumanu School the white-columned building seemed enormous. Without Mama for support, I needed to report my string of absences to the office. Retreating into passive silence, I stood in the main hallway in front of the office with its impressive counter, convinced I was in trouble. The dark paneling and polished wood flooring came together into a tunnel of cool air where important things happened, and people spoke in official whispers.

Hanging high on the wall against the painted white wood, positioned to face the person entering up the broad steps through the columned entrance was a large portrait of Queen Kaʻahumanu, our school's namesake. Someone had placed an offering bouquet of many-colored flowers under the picture. I studied her fully fleshed face, the insignia of rank in the background and her guarded expression. In return her eyes reviewed me, a small girl who wasn't sure what to do next.

As I stalled and paced the corridor, the morning bell rang, and all the other children disappeared. Alone in my patch of indecision, with flashing eyes, I mapped out how and where I would run if I had to. I balanced on one bare foot and then the other, while I studied the ancient lady's clear-eyed regard.

When Mrs. Kealoha-Henry found me, she laughed in surprise.

"So you did come back. And now you have met the Queen. Do you know her story? No? Well, I didn't think so."

The principal, a plump woman who wore old-fashioned glasses which dangled from a neckpiece onto the front of her shirtwaist, told me then and there about Queen Kaʻahumanu, the *Kuhina Nui.* I learned that she was a favorite child and a favorite wife, that her hair was called *ehu,* meaning it was reddish unlike that of other Hawaiians of her time, and that she was *hapa*—of mixed blood, probably from Spanish ancestors. Mrs. Kealoha-Henry suspected the conquistadores, whose helmets the Hawaiian *alii* had copied in feathers, had been the first Europeans in Hawaiʻi. I heard the kindly stranger saying that I, too, must be *hapa.* To test me she tried out some Hawaiian, and when I answered correctly, "*Aloha kakahiaka,*" she nodded favorably. She suggested a visit to the school library, where I would be welcome to read more about the

Queen and what she did with the tremendous power she held at the end of her life.

Mrs. Kealona-Henry put her hands on my shoulders and turned me in the direction of the polished *koa* wood steps that led to the second floor. She would take care of the absences.

Although I hoped that the principal had not confused me with someone else who was Hawaiian by blood, I was very pleased with the thrilling story. Her comments became the bond between the Queen and me. I felt lucky that I went to a school where a *hapa* was the boss—in fact, commanded tribute. After all, I did have the reddish hair, or some of it, and if I was *hapa* as she said, then that was the reason for my being different from the others. I felt lighter whenever I looked at Queen Ka'ahumanu's portrait from then on. Every day the Queen's round face gave me a signal that I was okay: a small thing, but necessary for someone so hungry for a sign.

Still, no matter how hard I squinted, the hair depicted in the painting showed no sign of being red. Never mind, I told myself, she was right there, up high, and she looked at me affectionately, if I kept up the squint. Whenever I needed to, I found my way back to the hallway to stand in the breeze and acknowledge the power of our kinship.

I had singled out Darleen Nishimura, a sixth grader, as my new model. I wanted to grow up to look just like her, even though she despised me.

Darleen looked so dainty and petite as she completed every action with grace. I tagged along behind her as she received smiles and praises, followed her as she delivered newspapers for her older brothers. But when she saw me, she looked annoyed and tried to shake me. She often escaped by cutting through a yard unknown to me. She made a clippety-clop sound with her merry flopping slippers, a sound which left you with a carefree rhythm. When she laughed, she covered her teeth delightfully with a hand in the way some of the older Japanese women did. I practiced and got nowhere. Never mind that Darleen wouldn't give me the time of day. Now I could forget it. Queen Ka'ahumanu was somber and regal; she never giggled.

One day I spotted another girl, this one chubby and my own age, standing in front of the painting. She quickly placed a white ginger blossom on the *koa* table and disappeared with a smile at me. Later, I heard her name was Monica. When we played in the school yard together, she revealed the secret of her full name: Monica Mahealani Michiko Macadangdang. Happily memorizing it on the spot, I learned that choosing friends wasn't the only way you got them; some chose you, if you were lucky.

Midway through the year I was happy enough to be going to school there, skipping down the streets extra early, eager to help water the taro patch and the red and gold lilies.

Three years later I was a bonafide Ka'ahumanu Kid, as accustomed as any one of my classmates to the school routine. Our neighbor Mrs. Lee, who lived on our block, must have seen my enthusiasm. She entrusted her only son, who had been living in Makawao, Maui, to my care since we were both in the fourth grade. Joseph and I walked to school together on his first day.

I felt a nudge from one side and a soft pinch from the other.

Just before the first morning bell rang, the whispers traveled around. We were aware that our teacher was moving down the line to study each one of us. Our voices were high, and our faces as busy as the noisy birds in the banyan outside. Always chattering, always in tune with our buddies, always watching, we knew how to move together on our quiet bare feet, without getting caught talking. We studied how to do it.

"Pssssssst . . ."

"Joseph. Make quick. We gotta line up; no talk. Standupstraight. Sing loud or she gon' make us guys sing one mo' time."

"She checking da guys' clothes first, if clean or what. Bumbye she gon' look our finganail and den check our hair behind da eah, l'dat."

The clanging bell brought us to silent attention.

Joseph looked completely blank. Unconcerned, he, being new, had no understanding of the importance of our morning classroom ritual. He didn't even pretend to mouth the words of Mrs. Vincente's favorite greeting, "Good Morning, Deah Tea-cha, Goooood Mor-ning to Youuu."

"W'at fo' she like check us in da eah?" Joseph's slow whisper tickled.

Before I could answer importantly, 'Cuz got *ukus*, some guys, you stupid doo-doo head," and think, "But not us guys," our teacher was standing right in front of us. Mrs. Vincente looked grim. Her gold-rimmed eyeglasses gave off glints in the pools of sunlight, evidence of real daylight outside, which invaded our dark, high-ceilinged and wood-paneled classroom.

She was the one who taught us to sing "Old Plantation *Nani Ole*" (Oooll . . . Plan-tay-shun . . . Na-ni . . . Ohlay) and "Ma-sa's (never her way, Massa's) in the Cold, Cold Ground," her favorite mournful melodies. She had turned to making us sing in order to drill us on our English skills, so lacking were we in motivation.

Frequently Mrs. Vincente spoke sharply to us about the inappropriate silences of our group. She complained that too often we spoke out of turn but "rarely contributed to the discussion." She must have believed that we didn't absorb anything that she lectured about repeatedly. She confided that she was "disappointed in" us or we had "disappointed Teacher" or she was "sorry to have to disappoint" us, "however," we had done something wrong again.

She was a puzzle.

The oriental kids—for that was our label—in the room knew better than to open their mouths just to lose face, and the part-Hawaiian and Portuguese kids knew they would get lickings one way or another if they talked, so we all firmly agreed that silence was golden.

Never would an adult female loom up as large to me as Mrs. Vincente did then. I could see her face only when I sat at a safe distance with a desk for protection. If she approached—in all her girth she was most graceful moving across her neatly waxed floor—her hands took my complete attention. When they were ready to direct us, I felt the way I did when Mama showed me what the red light at the crosswalk was for. When Teacher stood very near me, I couldn't see her tiny eyes, because the soft underpart of her delicate chin transfixed me so that I could not understand the words she mouthed. I got my mouth wrenched up to be ready for an alert answer, just in case she eyeballed me. Somehow whenever I had to respond to her I managed to get the subject and verb unmatched—"Yes, ma'am. We is ready fo' class"—even though she drilled us on the continual sin of the mixed singular and plural, because it was so fascinating to see her furious reaction to what she called Broken English, which none of us could fix.

Passing outside by Room 103, I overheard her passionate argument with another teacher who wanted to introduce the hula in our PE exercises. Mrs. V.'s reasoning escaped me, but I knew she was against it unconditionally. I stayed hidden in the *ti* leaves under her window just to hear the rush of her escaping emotions as she grew angrier and pronounced words more distinctly.

Mrs. Vincente's face was averted from the horrors she saw represented in the existence of our whole class. To her, we were not by any means brought up well, didn't know our p's and q's, often acted in an un-American fashion as evidenced by our smelly home lunches, dressed in an uncivilized manner, and refused moreover to speak properly or respectfully as soon as her back was turned. Her standards were in constant jeopardy.

Our concentrated looks centered on her totally. We followed her every move, a fact which unnerved her briefly each morning. To hide her discomfort, revealed by streams of perspiration, she swabbed her face delicately with a lace-trimmed hankie.

She shook her head at Francene Fuchigami, whose mother made her wear around her neck an amulet in a yellowed cotton pouch which also contained a foul incense and active herbs. The blessed *o-mamori* guaranteed the absence of both slippery vermin and casual friends.

Francene and I competed for Mrs. V.'s favor, no matter how much we accepted her obvious but peculiar interest in the boys only. She favored them shamelessly, but bullied them at every opportunity.

We brought Mrs. Vincente homegrown anthuriums, tangerines and sticky notes: "Dear Mrs. V., Your so nice. And your so pretty, too," with high hopes. *Maybe she will like me now,* ran the thread of wishful thinking. Winning her favor took all of my attention. I had to stay neat and clean and pretend to be a good girl, somebody who could "make nice-nice" and "talk high *maka-mak.*" To win Mrs. Vincente over, I saw that I would have to be able to speak properly, a complicated undertaking demanding control of all my body parts, including my eyes and hands, which wandered away when my mouth opened up. Therefore, in a compromise with my desire to shine, I resolved to keep absolutely quiet, stand up with the stupid row and ignore the one I wanted to impress.

Mrs. Vincente was one of us, she claimed, because she herself had grown up in our "very neighborhood." Her school, too, she once let out, had been non-English Standard. We were surprised to hear her say that her family was related to the Kahanus who owned the corner grocery store. We knew them, the ones who used to have money. The brothers Eugene and Franklin Teves claimed they knew for sure she couldn't be kin to anyone they recognized, in answer to the other class who called her "The Portagee Teacha." She spoke, dressed and carried herself in a manner that was unlike any of the women I observed at home, but she fit right in with our other teachers who, like her, had gone to Normal School and shared her authoritative ways.

Difficult as she was, we could understand her preoccupation. Getting rid of *ukus* was a tedious job connected with beratings from your mother and lickings from your father. We always knew who carried *ukus* and were swift to leave that child alone. News traveled fast. All the same we could each remember what it felt like to be the "odd man out," which was the name of one of our favorite games.

To have *ukus*, to tell your close friends not to tell the others, and to have them keep the secret: that was the test of friendship. Like the garbage men who worked under the *uku pau* system, which meant that no gang or worker was finished until everybody on that truck helped the final guy unload his very last can, and everybody could quit, *uku* season wasn't over until every kid got rid of every last clinging egg.

At Christmastime, Mrs. Vincente wrapped up a useful comb for each and every one of us. At the end of the year we raced each other to be the first one lined up at her massive desk.

We would each shyly request her autograph with the suggested correct phrases, "Please, Mrs. Vincente," and "Thank you, Teacha," so she must have been what we had grown to expect a teacher to be.

Because of Mrs. Vincente I wanted to become a teacher. I wanted to wield power and know how to get my way. I wanted to be the one who would point out a minute, luminous silver egg sack stuck on a coarse black hair, shake it vigorously with arm held out far away from body, and declare victoriously, "Infestation . . . of . . . pediculosis!"

She would then turn to address the entire class. "This child must go directly to the nurse's office." She would speak firmly but in a softer tone to the kid. "Do not return to our room until you can bring me the white clearance certificate signed by both of your parents."

Completely silent during class, I practiced those words at home while I played school. I turned to the class. I gave the warning to the kid. Mrs. Vincente was not to be taken lightly.

The day Joseph learned about *ukus*, I figured out teachers.

Facing him, Mrs. Vincente demanded to know the new boy's name from his own mouth.

"Joseph Kaleialoha Lee."

"Say ma'am."

"Hah?"

"You must say 'Joseph Kaleialoha Lee, ma'am.'"

"Joseph-Kaleialoha-Lee-ma'am!"

"Hold out your hands, please."

Evidently he had not paid attention, the biggest error of our collective class, one which we heard about incessantly. He had not watched her routine, which included a search for our hidden fingernail dirt. He held his hands palms up. I shuddered.

Mrs. Vincente studied Joseph with what we called the "stink eye," but he still didn't catch on. She must have considered his behavior insubordinate, because he did not seem retarded or neglected as he was wearing his new long, khaki pants and a freshly starched aloha shirt.

She reached into the big pocket of her apron and took out a fat wooden ruler. Our silence was audible. She stepped up a little nearer to Joseph, almost blocking out all the air and light around us so that her sharp features and steely voice cut through to reach our wobbly attention.

"What grade are you in now, young man?"

Joseph was silent as if in deep thought. Why wouldn't he say the answer? I nudged him quickly on his side with the hand nearest his body.

"Fot grade," he blurted in a small, panicky wheeze.

She turned on us all, enraged at our murmurs of anticipation. We knew for sure he would get it now.

Some girl giggled hysterically in a shrill whinny. "Heengheengheeng . . ." Probably Japanese.

"Quiet."

Businesslike, she returned to Joseph with her full attention, peering into his ear. "Say th, th, th. Speak slowly." He heard the warning in her voice.

"Tha, tha, tha." Joseph rippled droplets of sweat.

"Th, th, th . . . everyone, say it all together: the tree!"

We practiced loudly with Joseph leading the chorus, relieved now to be part of the mass of voices.

"Say the tree, not da chree."

"The tree, not da chree."

"Fourth grade, not fot grade."

"Foth grade, not foth grade."

With a rapid searching movement which caught most of us off guard, Mrs. Vincente swung around to face Darcie Ah Sing, whose hand was still stuck in her curly brown hair when she was spotted scratching herself vigorously. Mrs. V. stared blackly into Darcie's tight curls with unshakeable attention. In a matter of seconds, with an upward swoop of her palm, Teacha found the louse at the nape of the exposed neck and pronounced her memorable conclusion, ending with "by both of your parents," indicting Darcie's whole family into the crime.

"March yourself into the office, young lady." Mrs. Vincente wrung a hankie between her pudgy hands with tight motions. Head hanging, Darcie moved out wordlessly to the school nurse's station for the next inspection. We knew that she would be "shame" for a long time and stared at our dusty toes in hopeless sympathy.

When we were allowed to sit at our desks (after practicing the sks sound for desks: "sssk'sss, sssk'sss, dehss-kuss, dehss-kuss, dehss-kuss, not desses, dessess, dessess"), we were hooked into finishing our tasks of busywork and wearing our masks of obedience, totally subdued.

Then she read to us, as she explained that she was "wont to do when the occasion arose," while we sat at our desks with our hands folded quietly as she had trained us. She enunciated each word clearly for our benefit, reminding us that by the time we graduated we would be speaking "proper English" and forgot the *uku* check for the day. Her words stuck like little pearly grains into the folds of my brain. I pondered how to talk *haole* while she continued to lecture.

"The child . . . the school . . . the tree . . ." I could not hear the meaning of her words and scratched my head idly but in secret, my head dodging her line of vision. I yearned to master her knowledge, but dared not make myself the target of her next assault. I was not getting any smarter, but itchier by the minute, more eager than anyone to break free into the oasis of recess.

When the loud buzzer finally shattered the purring motor of her voice, we knew better than to whoop and scatter. We gathered our things formally and waited silently to be dismissed. If we made noise we would have to sit inside in agony, paying attention to the whole endless, meaningless story which sounded like all the ones before and wasted our precious time. Even Joseph caught on.

He said, "Whew, 'as waste time."

Once we were outside, surveying the situation, we saw two teams of the bigger boys who pulled at a heavy knotted rope from opposite ends. Joseph's bare feet dug into the ground right in back of Junior Boy, the tug-of-war captain. Clearly he wouldn't need any more of my guidance if Junior Boy had let him in. Beads of wetness sparkled off their bodies as the tight chain of grunting boys held fast under the bright sun.

Noisy clumps of kids skipped rope and kicked up the grass, twisting bodies and shining faces, all together in motion. Racing around the giant banyan, for no good reason, I scream-giggled, "Wheeeeeha-ha-hah!" Like a wildcat I roared up the trunk of the chree . . . just to see if I could.

Joseph spotted me. "Too good, you!" he yelled.

While the girls played jacks, and the boys walked their board stilts, Joseph and I moved around groups trading milk bottle covers and playing marbles. We wondered aloud to each other. We spread the word.

"Ho, w'atchoo tink?"

"Must be da teacha wen' catch *ukus* befo'."

"Not . . ."

"Not not!"

"Cannot be . . ."

"Can can!"

"Yeah?"

"Ay, yeah. O' how else she can spock 'em dat fast?"

That made me laugh, the thought of Mrs. V. picking through her careful topknot. She would have to moosh away the hibiscus to get in a finger. I mimed her by scratching through the hair I let hang down in front of my face. When I swept it back professionally with the palm of my hand, I threw in a cross-eyed crazy look. Joseph pretended to "spock *uku*" in my hair as he took on Mrs. V's exaggerated ladylike manner to hold onto one of my ears like a handle and peer into the endless *puka*.

"Ho, man," he proclaimed, "get so planny inside."

The recess bell rang, ending our sweet freedom. We pranced back to the classroom in a noisy herd. Teacha gave us the Look. We grew cautious. We would spend the next hour silently tracking Mrs. Vincente's poised head, while Joseph and I smiled knowingly at each other.

Eyes gleaming, Mrs. Vincente never disappointed any of us, because she always stuck right on her lessons and never let up at all. She stayed mean as ever, right on top of the class. As for us, fourth grade *ukus* could appreciate the effort . . . so much not letting go.

*M*ust have been '52. On New Year's Eve when Sparky Takahashi was maybe twelve and I was nine, he set the canefield on fire at the H.S.P.A. That means the Hawaii Sugar Planters Association which is all gone from Makiki now. Finally.

Spark had a lot of impetigo over his dark, skinny legs and arms. He sported one wild popeye and plenty of hair, short but thick. When the cane was blazing, something which the lane kids never expected since it was mostly green, he showed us he could run like hell.

Siren and all, the police came right away to Makiki Court. It was off Makiki Street, in the lower valley, the little lane running down the middle of about a dozen plantation bungalows and winding up to one big, carved-up mansion in the back by the wooden garage shed. Our gang led the way, but the officers already knew where Spark lived. They rapped on the screen door of his house. Turned out they were the two heavyset cops. One was tall, Chinese-Hawaiian, and the other short, with a Filipino name, who always kept at least one eye open wide over all the neighborhood children.

Sparky was scared, but he couldn't lie or run away easily since we were all hanging around the edge of the porch watching to see what would happen and if they were going to take him to the station to beat him up. We used to tease him, "Spock you laters," and wink because of the name Sparky. But we said nothing about seeing him now. Nobody even wanted to lie for him, to say he wasn't the one setting off skyrockets over there, because he never let anybody touch his stuff, not even look at one of his small cherry bombs. We knew he had them when he showed off by guarding his bulging Hawaiian Air flight bag. He always acted cocky, but he was just like everybody else.

I was thinking, "Good for you, Sparky. Now you gon' catch it."

Mr. Takahashi was holding him by the back of the neck. His voice was sighing and squeaking when he told the police, "I wen' find him unda da bed. Ho, bad egg, dis one."

Mr. Takahashi was always calm, but what a thing to say about his own son. Maybe he thought they would let him off that way. Spark looked like a fish with his mouth open, body squirming, arms trying to flap away, so maybe he couldn't even hear what the grownups were saying.

"Take him station. Teach him one lesson." Mr. Takahashi looked like a stern demon with bushy eyebrows. He had the eyes that bugged out too. Even the new crowd in the lane, real outsiders who came to see what kind of accident it was, could tell right off it was a father-son case.

But the old man was sharp. He acted like he was going to turn the boy over to Officer Kawelo, the easy cop. One time, quick, he made like he wen' shove Spark to him, but he aimed his body right through the two men. Big guys, fumbling around, they couldn't catch what happened.

"Huh? Hold it right hea, boy."

Slippery Sparky went for the chance. Officer Calaro tried, but he could only hold on to the back pocket, which got ripped off from the rest of the moving body. Down the steps, shoving Old Lady Machado to one side, stepping on Dennis's baby sister and pushing right through the neighbor's bushes, Spark took off. Before you could spit on the ground, we couldn't see him at all. He knew it would take too long for the slow fats to charge him. Plus he had the advantage at night.

We jumped, whooping, off the railing and ran after our friend.

"Spock you later. Good one!" He was a wild buggah, and we had a feeling he would show up down the stream. What a bimbo-chimpo. By now I was hoping he would make it.

Officer Calaro put his finger into his khaki shirt collar to loosen the necktie. Calaro was angry at the father, grumbling to him, "You send him over tomorrow, yeah?" He gave all of us the real *kukae* stink eye, as if we did something, and he smelled it too.

People started to go home, back to the partying. You could hear firecrackers from up and down Makiki Street and popping sounds from the little yards in the Court. Back in their Dodge cruiser, Kawelo and Calaro took off to someplace else, maybe a roadblock for drunks, but they were quiet about it. Mr. Takahashi was behind his screen door again looking in the direction of the burned-out section of cane across the street. Some Filipino working men were still hosing down the part of the fence that had been burned. A fine rain from the cloudy sky helped out: *pio*, it was over. Everything looked like normal, except for the night, which was smoking red with fumes and once in a while, the fiery streak of a skyrocket. Somebody up in Tantalus had some real good ones going.

We would find Spark later when things got slow. New Year's was the big event, the thing we knew was coming from the time we smelled Christmas around the corner.

Now I can remember how much I ran around in those old baby days. I was whatever the day was. I marked the pace with my whole body, breathing in and out to step up a good chase from sunup to day's end. I was in a hurry to taste it all. I flicked our house radio from the Cherry Blossom Hour to Boston Blackie to Hawaii Calls' Tropic Melodies, dancing by myself to every lively voice and tune. And I waited for New Year's with unbearable patience.

Best of all was seeing my mother's husband drunk under the bed. Duffy would always hide there. I would count on him. The patter of firecrackers drove him wild as he headed for cover, remembering the flying bullets from the war that haunted his brain.

I watched her beat him with a wire hanger.

"Stand up like one man!"

I watched him turn into a screaming child. He was a gutless wonder. She would be crying too. She had no brain. At those times I disappeared into the closet, walls, furniture. I was completely still, just a camera waiting. A skinny girl with big eyes.

When I had enough of them, I escaped back to the Court and the action around me. New Year's Eve was when I could count on a rhythm to meet my own, to swirl me on my way. The night was fast.

The sound of firecrackers whizzed and rip-popped through the air.

"Look up!"

Just before disintegration there was still the last colorful image frozen in watery aerial action, trailing fancy tails and shrieking whistles. Occasional rapid fire popping just down our street made me take notice of the ground. All the small animals, down to the last nervous mongoose, were suddenly burrowed in, hidden somewhere tight. They shuddered to the rat-a-tat of a tiny string of crackers, followed by the thunder of an explosion in a garbage can. Familiar cats were nowhere. Smoke was heavy everywhere, hiding the excited scurries of movement in the night air. Familiar people looked like strangers, dark figures in milky darkness, moving wildly. They danced around flames on the cement. Fluorescent colors flashed, and gold was molten in red-flame. Night jewels decorated our patches of grass while the whole edgy town reveled.

Somebody's father, a big guy, shimmied up to string a long rope into a telephone pole eyelet hook. Small children, jumping up and down in excitement beneath him, willed the entire setup. The firecrackers hung down six feet in a braid that almost reached the sidewalk. One of the younger uncles held out a burning match. Instantly everyone cleared away.

"Ha ha. Only kidding." He flicked the flaring sliver into the gutter.

This string was saved for the main attraction, ready for the moment it would become the midnight marker.

So much going on! I couldn't stand waiting. I hopped in a tight circle, hugging myself, waiting for the final explosion of the whole night fabric, when the crackling roar would erupt through the entire island. Light, color, noise, voices, and feeling would surge through all the living and even ripple out to touch some ideas that we thought were gone. Time was still. Everything melded into the general breathless waiting in the midst of so much sound. Even I was forced to anchor myself to quietness.

I spotted a cockroach. ll:57 p.m. Driven into a frenzy by the constant din, it zigzagged around my feet, going for the telephone pole where the chunky line dangled. The roach looked like an overburdened Dodge, rocking back and forth, bent for somewhere out of the exploding light. It stopped short just in front of the pole. A quivering roach drunk with noise.

Leaping, I stepped on it. Crunch, slide. It was no longer afraid. But I shrieked and fell backwards, catching myself and racing up to our porch steps. I saw Monica's uncle's hand reach out to set the long fuse on fire.

"Covahup yo' eahs," she screeched at me.

Nineteen fifty-two left us in a roar, "Happy New Yeah!" The adults continued drinking, feeling good. Somebody shot off a gun, "Wheehah!" Voices were singing. Radios turned up louder. The lane was violently alive, a distillation of our vibrance.

I saw it in red, yellow and black: the rocky new beginning. *Pachi-pachi-pachi* echoed on through the rest of the dark hours into the morning.

When everyone thought we were asleep, we met by our marble ring in the dirt next to Spark's wash house. Some of the kids couldn't escape their families or their need to sleep. So three of us got set to search the stream to find Spark.

Lee and David were older and expected another boy, Wyn Silva, not me. Monica and I were going to be the tag-alongs, but she couldn't get out of her house. That left me. They were not happy about letting me stay.

"Okay. You, girl! Go home now. Beat it. Go sleep."

"Lemme see, too. Come on, you folks . . . otherwise I-going-to-tell."

I tailed them as we ran to the garbage pit in the back of all the sheds and apartments. There was an open space and a barbed wire fence before the hillside slouched down to the stream.

The stream divided us from the places where *haoles* would care to live. They lived up in the bungalows at Punahou Cliffs and at Arcadia, which was home for a governor. I was in awe of that vast lawn. The mysteries of a manicured lotus pond and a weathered barn could lure me across the stream. People on that side had cocktail parties in slow motion and drank to the sound of tinkling ice and bubbling laughter. Some of them spread out beach towels to sunbathe by the hour. I had seen this myself, passing very near and silent in the glittering water.

As soon as we were there standing above the stream on the stone embankment, Lee made the owl sounds which would alert Spark to us. There was no answer.

We knew he was hiding in the tunnel.

Lee and I had to go first since I had the flashlight.

"But David already took 'um, and I wearing only slippahs."

"Go home, chicken!"

I looked down at my feet, too scared to face the command to retreat. They decided they needed me then. David pushed the light back to me. The two of them made me walk ahead, instructing me to play the beam on the ground and the sliding dirt of the rocky slope. We held on to the roots of the big banyan at the edge of the canal. It guided us down.

Once we were next to the water, the mouth of the tunnel gaped ahead. The arch wasn't higher than ten feet, but we had seen mountain water gushing through it, flooding it completely in a short time, and I had been warned to stay away from the bums and escaped convicts that were sure to be hiding in there. My own eyes had seen whiskey bottles discarded on ledges within the recesses of the first part of the tunnel. I never went further. The others were sure the tunnel would come out in Waikiki past Pawa'a Theater. Monica used to insist it would lead to the ocean at the end of the canal.

My nose told me it was a place of decay which waste water itself could not wash away. I believed my mother who said it was filled with rat piss. My hesitating feet were saying the no that my mouth could not. Or maybe I just didn't talk much in those days. The worst thing of all would be to find Duffy drinking in there. He had many hiding places, so I couldn't count the tunnel out. I didn't want to think about him. Quietly I had edged back until the three of us were walking side by side. I wasn't going first.

The mossy slime on the concrete flooring which carried the stream bottom away from Makiki was trouble to walk on. The color under the flashlight's moving arc changed from green to brown. Reddish parts of it, which made the tunnel sides look bloody, seemed to be rusty scum water from metal feeder pipes leading out of the dirty culvert walls.

That night there wasn't much real water at all, just the little that lapped in from the stream at our back and tugged us further and further. The slow, oozing water licked at our feet. I began to feel closed in and looked backwards often to make sure the opening was still there. Forward, the light showed more orange greyness from the walls lined at their sides by debris of every kind. Silt gathered in places where sickly weeds grew.

We could hear the faint sounds of a trickling waterfall somewhere deeper ahead. Where we were had a hollow quiet.

"W'addat?"

David stopped. Lee moved wildly, ready to run backwards.

I froze, holding the light the way a statue would point a torch.

A rat skittered away on a ledge above our heads. I saw fierce red eyes which stayed suspended in my mind like the sky-rockets a few hours before.

David whistled through his teeth in disgust. He did it again louder.

And then we thought we heard Sparky answer us. A half whistle, maybe a wheeze.

We ran toward the sound, carefully avoiding hunks of bent metal, a rotten ironing board, broken bottles, and suspicious clumps of obscure rubbish. We passed too near an almost forgotten and deep crevice which held the unspoken rumor of polio water, the illness our mothers forever threatened us with, if they didn't mention our getting sores, real *kakius* on our legs.

"Ova hea!" Lee yelled into the darkness.

"Hea, hea . . . " bounced off the tunnel in echoes. For a long time we moved nearer and nearer the outfall's patter. The light marked a hump in the wall.

When we saw him up in the niche, he looked like somebody else.

I flashed the beam directly on the crouching figure. Suddenly someone next to it moved up jerkily, half awake.

"Annudah guy. Two."

He leered confused into the light, his head cocked at a strange angle.

"Damn *pilute*. You piss drunk."

I felt so much shame that I looked down into the wet darkness lapping at my feet.

David hisssed scornfully. It was his brother Larry, and Larry's sidekick, the high school boy with a mustache. They had been drinking beer in their secret place.

Seeing who the others saw, the slow recognition brought me only a flicker of relief that it wasn't Duffy, after all.

When Larry realized who we were, accusing him with our light, he pelted us with beer bottles. He was furious but a junk shot. I dodged. He missed me, too. In panic I dropped the flashlight. There was no time to feel for it, to regret the licking I would get for losing it.

Then we were racing again, back to the tunnel entrance, hoping in cold perspiration to avoid the dark traps along the way. David's brother's fury followed us in echoes. We could hear bottles hitting the tunnel wall and the echoing of the hits and the glass falling like smashed rain.

It was a long run.

My heart felt alive again when I finally saw the opening and passed through it immediately to scramble up the dirt hillside in murky, mottled moonlight.

There was air. The banyan roots felt like a lifeline. The heaving relief of coming up lightened me, the last one out.

It was when we reached over the top of the wall, when our muddy feet touched the ground on the other side, that we heard the laughter. Spark was cackling at us from his nest high in the tree. He thought we were funny. He tilted his head back as he brayed and coughed and howled at us. He couldn't stop.

I was still puffing and too ready to bolt for home. I couldn't figure it out fast.

"Eh, jaggass, come on down hea," Lee shouted, ready to fight him.

Spark laughed even more, sputtering and heehawing.

Looking for him, I saw his bent silhouette above crotch of the tree. His head up higher looked trapped by the branches. He began to make his way down.

I was thinking. He played a joke on us. He made me scared. Sparky and Duffy were the same, two of a kind. My anger flooded over me, and my voice found its way out, pushing past tightly held-in tears and the fearful caution which kept me silent.

I spluttered, "I gon' squash you, good for notting lo-lo."

When I went for him to obliterate him with my flailing hands and arms and feet, Lee and David had to drag me back, still choking angry. They had watched Spark's useless foot come down first. It was wrapped up in a bloody T-shirt.

Standing painfully, Spark had to straighten his left side slowly. While in the tunnel he had stepped on a hidden jag of glass.

He spoke to me.

"Joking, okay?"

And his eyes were looking into me. I had never seen myself that way before, reflected in someone's eyes.

I looked small and hopeless.

Somehow I got home, tearfully running away from those miserable boys and sleeping long into the first day of the New Year, forgetting the endless tunnel and the gashed foot, the fire and the anger.

Spark's punishment, my lickings, Lee and David, the whole Court disintegrated slowly until years later I could not remember that they were once part of me. Until I applied a tint of burnt ocher on the palette and found some old green crayon, I thought only about the fire. The green brought back a memory of water.

The day before I had gone to help Monica's mother in her 10' x 10' Makiki Park garden. Mrs. Macadangdang went home to feed her invalid husband who waited alone in their high rise apartment. He sometimes sat by a window watching the tiny figures—us this time—moving around on the ground. I was digging sweet potatoes. Crouched down, dripping with sweat, I found out how the earth casually resists the would-be farmer's hand. No longer the H.S.P.A. headquarters, the ground was city property now. In the middle of softening the soil, I had stepped on a sharp spear of growing sugar cane. A hard green thing. It was still sending out stray shoots in the desperate way of a crop that has been banished from its former field.

The stomach of my foot ached.

When I hopped over to a water faucet, I saw the Filipino man. I opened up the spigot to bathe the sore foot and watched with interest as the stranger swung a pickax against the brick wall of an old laboratory.

Like a few other structures, the remnant had already been emptied and abandoned, but the three walls, two of them wooden, maintained their old experiment station form. Bit by bit the heavy wall was crumbling, chink echoing after thump, with every blow.

The hardy old goat did not let up. His face glistened with moisture. All of the energy of his being concentrated on tearing down the wall. As he flailed and hacked, he grunted and swore continuously. He stopped to sing a version of *The Star-Spangled Banner.* Was he insane? Stone drunk: He looked like somebody's grandfather with all his shirt buttons neatly fastened.

I was too embarrassed to stick around or reveal my fascination. I returned to digging and heard him laughing joyously to himself.

When noontime arrived he was still at work. The sun set him afire with its glow and heat.

When I picked up my hoe and hose, ready to go home for the sweltering afternoon, only half the red wall was broken down. My discouraged eye found his face and scanned the unfinished work once more.

"Those bricks are for the garden?" I asked him and pointed at the rubble at his feet and then waved toward the plots. Some gardeners set up little boundaries and stepping stones in their areas.

The man got up from his squatting rest, straightening himself full length, his back to the glare.

He shook his head and wiped the sweat off his face with a handkerchief. He blew his nose.

When he was done he looked directly at me and smiled kindly.

"It is just time for this building to come down. If you wish, you may have the leftovers. I used to work in this place here as a laborer."

He turned away and continued to bring the wall down. His action made me remember Makiki Court and the way it was.

"No . . . can . . . help . . . ." He released a word with each flashing whack and laughed again.

*O*h boy, oh boy. Quick. Come ova hea, Monica! Ho, dis place real nice, yeah?

I peered into a beige living room through an open window above the manicured green lawn where we had been throwing leaping cartwheels. The window right next to it was still firmly closed and darkened by straggly cobwebs.

"Yeah, man. And look ova dea at da big fiaplace. What dey going do wid all dose nuspepas?"

Leading our eyes up to the high ceiling, piles of tied up papers waited for some kind of action.

"Mebbe dey gon' use'm for make da fi-a."

We saw a large figure slouched into a plush arm chair. She, for although she wore

THE GIFT

men's clothing, a faded oversized aloha shirt tucked into men's starched pants, and studied a newspaper, then us, through metal frame bifocals, was Mrs. Withamm. The neighborhood recluse, "the lady with da whiskas" beckoned us into her strange living quarters. Strange because her front door was boarded up and no one ever saw her during the day. Only a crew of Filipino yard men worked on her yard, the only human figures we saw on her spacious property.

Monica and I looked at each other and shrugged, *Oh, why not?* We knew about her. She was lo-lo. It was safe.

One foot on the outside house trim, one after another, we pushed up and wriggled right in like eels squirming into a new part of the ocean.

She stood up formally. She watched us carefully. A gracious hostess, she offered us old Christmas candy, sourballs and hard bits on a fancy plate, which we took happily, each of us jamming several sticky nuggets in our mouths at once. She placed one in her mouth, sucking thoughtfully. She motioned us to sit.

We sat ourselves down with care to do it properly on a sheet-covered sofa. Our brown feet stuck out in front of us, too busy to stay quiet, unused to the thick carpet. Our arms and hands, too, suddenly run out of activity to keep them busy, made tight uneasy motions. Monica and I grew antsy in the concentration of silence. We could smell the oldness rising up everywhere. Monica sneezed. We looked at each other and giggled. We held hands which got sticky and then let go. We dangled our limbs and stared back at the lady silently. Waiting.

She was suddenly above our faces. Peering at us from a standing position, she clasped her hands together and beamed her pleasure.

"Ah, good!"

We startled, ready to bolt. Monica turned her gaze back to check the open window. I was transfixed by the bifocaled gray eyes. A little line of perspiration materialized out of the humid air, and my upper lip grew heavier as I stared at her very close but only occasional facial hairs.

"My blessed little girl had hair like yours. Would you like to hear how she died?"

We shook our heads yes, no, yes. We eyed each other in confusion. In the end it was her conversational tone which kept us there, ready for the story. She was so sure that we would be interested, and so we stayed.

Each chance we could leave Makiki Court unnoticed we came back to hear more about the adored baby. There was nothing so exciting at our homes. She was named Jeannie Joanne, sometimes "blessed" and sometimes "darling." She had red hair and was only a toddler when she died in her mother's arms. We wept a few soft tears the first time we heard of this, but the story changed too many times. The only words that stayed the same were "and she died in my arms, my little pretty one. My blessed Jeannie Joanne."

On our first visit Mrs. W., for that is how she instructed us to call her, showed us little dead Jeannie Joanne's bedroom. A tiny bed covered with a fine quilt stood against the far wall. A delicate blue silk sofa was placed next to it in such a way that anyone sitting in it could lean right over the bed. The furniture in the room was old, we could tell that, and very much taken care of. The colors, too, were eggshell and robin's egg blue, not that we had ever seen the bird. She told us everything.

"No master bedroom at all," announced Mrs. W.

I explained to Monica that it was just like Mama and how she thought about men after all the trouble she got from Duffy. Only Mama told her nurse friends, "Listen, you don't need a man all the time, honey."

And we noticed that the bedroom was very different from the other rooms that we passed once we got up the stairs. It was a normal room whereas the others were filled with unusual piles that looked like heaps of rubbish. Later we learned that the piles were Mrs. W.'s special collection. They filled all the parts of her house except for Jeannie Joanne's blue bedroom and the portion of the living room in which Mrs. W. liked to keep guard over the house.

While we all felt so bad together in the baby's room, Monica made the mistake of asking to see her picture. Mrs. W. became very angry. Without telling us why she wouldn't let us see

Jeannie Joanne's photo, she changed the subject as adults did all the time. But why she stayed so angry was a mystery.

"And who are you? What is your name? I have never met your parents or yours either."

She turned to me with great annoyance.

As Monica stammered, "Monica Macadangdang, ma'am." I thought about the answers I was pressed for by curious adults and briefly weighed not saying anything but my name.

So I said it

"Lei . . . "

Mrs. W. took me in with a shiver and a scowl.

"So you have white blood in you. I can see that. Both of you as healthy as weeds, with no one watching after you or giving you any kind of vitamins."

She began to regret her words as we inched away from her.

"No, no, it's not your fault. You see, this fool of a doctor, my husband's friend, was the one who lanced a boil on her forehead, right smack in the middle. My precious baby. And you see, it hit the main blood vessel and the child was covered with blood which gushed out of her in such a startling way that she could barely cry. She was surprised and she weakened and she was dead almost immediately. I looked at her eyes and saw the terrible hurt draining all her life force. She was dead in the cradle of my arms."

But Mrs. W. had just told us that the darling baby had learned to walk and had wandered all by herself in the garden where she tumbled into the lily pond and drowned. Mrs. W. had discovered her missing only a few minutes later and jumped into the water to drag the lifeless baby out, just a few breaths too late. Monica and I had already looked out the second story window to see if we could spot the overgrown pond where lily pads choked life from the gray water and no flowers ever seemed to blossom. We couldn't see it from the side of the house that faced the street. We exchanged looks: we could always check it out later.

What was she saying? Was there more than one baby who died? I held on tight to the subject in the silence that signified she was done with the new story.

"But she neva' die in da docta's office and right afta dat dey wen' go play golf widout so much as a look at da little dead baby?"

Mrs. W's face stiffened.

"Well! Now you girls can come back over here later on."

Her signal was her way of getting rid of us. We could take a hint.

In the months to come we learned the many ways that the baby might have died. My favorite was the abduction, her word and my fantasy.

Somebody wanted Jeannie Joanne so very much that he crept into the house late one night and kidnapped her and broke her mother's heart. It was the only one of a dozen stories in which her mother couldn't say, ". . . and she died in my arms." In this one Mrs. W. had to say, ". . . and I longed to hold her little dear body in my arms once again, but she was gone forever. Jeannie Joanne."

Monica and I kept coming back for more of Mrs. W.'s creepy stories. Sometimes I think we wished we could have been loved so fiercely and mourned so deeply by such an adoring mother. Both of ours worked.

Other mothers asked what their kids did in the day. Our moms were more likely to ask if we took down the line of wash or in Monica's case if she took care of her little brothers. Once in a while we did, but we had much more interest in running over to Mrs. W.'s. Allowed to play with the meager lily pond water and concoct

mud pies studded with bright yellow fruit from Mrs. W's chinaberry trees, we studied the *haole* lady's ways. *Just checking.*

When I told Mama I talked to the lady, she wasn't worried
at all but announced that she had heard all about her.

"Watch out for dat one. Mrs. Yonemitsu tole me she wen'
put one curse on her husband because he fool around one girl-
friend lady. But *bachi* wen' land on da wife. She came *pupule.* 'As
why she stay inside all da time. And da husband move out, but he
like drive around for watch da house."

So Monica and I had a lot to discuss while we made the
mud cakes and kept a weather eye peeled for the old man to drive
by—we just wanted to see his face and go "Uuujiii"—or for Mrs. W.
to lean out of her window to talk to us. Once in a while she even
made us Kool Aid and handed us glasses of it through the kitchen
door opened a bare crack. We knew she kept a stack of the empty
Kool Aid envelopes next to rows of old bottles and cans.

It was like this. A light went on inside her head. When she
was okay it shined through her lively features. She told us she had
been a high school teacher which made sense judging from her
ways. That was when she was okay. When Mrs. W. was not, we stayed
away, because she would not show herself at all, even when we
called or knocked on the walls and the back door. We knew she
rattled around by herself, talking softly in the crevices of the old
house; we knew she was busy constantly, saving all sorts of things,
stuffing whole rooms full of fragile, arranged rubbish. Spooky, we
agreed. We knew that was not right. Her head filled with bits and
pieces of other times and other people, she couldn't keep *us* and
now straight.

Her stately house showed us signs of what used to be.
Like the old place, Mrs. W. kept up a few pockets of order, a
beautiful bedroom, an immaculate area around the fireplace, but

the other large spaces were crammed with piles of things, old clothes, stacks of empty tin cans, rows of empty bottles, paper boxes and endless stacks of papers: newspapers, letters, advertisements, and who knew what in every direction. She couldn't bear to part with anything she had once touched. Keeping all of the paper, used tinfoil or brown paper which came in to her from the grocery delivery boy or the mailman or her two adult children—an annoyed-looking young man and a sad-faced woman who sometimes appeared driving out of her garage in a shiny sedan—meant she had to sort and organize all of it so that it would never leave her home again.

I was used to seeing people save old junk stuff. O-Baban, too, like all the plantation old folks, saved empties. But she used cans and paper up almost immediately. Mrs. W. did not let anything go. Neither did she use it. Mrs. W. stored it. That was her work.

Monica and I spent time figuring out what kind of thing we might give her. We could bring her rubbish. Everybody put out loads of it, especially on rubbish day when people took out stacks, cans, sacks and bags full of leavings in every variety. We laughed to think that we could think of doing such a thing and also about how quickly we would be able to help her fill the entire house to the rafters with garbage.

"Ho, one load Christmas time or right afta New Yeah's and she's all finish. *Pau hana* time!"

But Monica pointed out the problem.

"She gon' look chru all dat junk and make us pack 'em back. No good dat kind." She put her finger under her nose. "Pee U."

Instead we brought her a sack of mountain apples from Auntie Annabelle Soares. She always gave lots.

Tiny and chewy, the deep red and fleshy whiteness of the fruit and the cool spongy texture of the watery pulp made the glistening apples good for two bites each.

Mrs. W. snatched them up.

"Oh, good."

And she ushered us through the backdoor into her kitchen, eagerly mooshing us on to chairs. She fixed us coffee with cream and sugar which we loved and we talked as Monica would remember, "j'like anybody . . . good fun, her."

A high window brought cool breezes into the cramped kitchen where Mrs. W. sat to drink her coffee. Her ritual sitting, brooding and occasional singing—it sounded like a radio with static—lasted exactly the morning. If the day grew too hot, she fanned herself vigorously. If rainy weather made things chilly, she pulled on the red sweater draped on the back of her chair.

"How come you 'no go work, make money, Mrs. W?" We said, "Missus Double-yew," which made us too giggily to pay attention.

"What's that? Is that what your parents teach you! Money isn't the only thing in life, lamb pie. No, no, there are finer things to consider by far. Among them is integrity. You can look it up and chew on it for a while.

"Over there, the blue dictionary, the fat one by the stove." She kept three altogether. Her name was written in each.

Mrs. Withamm became our reference librarian for words we didn't understand, for puzzles and blanks. We came to her without embarrassment to ask questions we couldn't at home. We took on large problems because she was likely to answer. She did her best to give us meanings or reasons or to fill in the mysterious ways of adults.

"My madda say we been poor, our family been poor, and we gon' be poor no matta w'at, 'cuz 'as how suppose to be. How come?

"What means dis men-stru-a-tion?"

"My Baban and Ji-chan no like talk wid my madda husband. Dey no like him. Dey no like talk wid my Mada, and she come sad. Mo' betta no mo husband, yeah?"

She insisted that we practice speaking with her and corrected our English by saying what we had said but changing patterns and words for us. She avoided making us feel stupid so it was not like school.

"You mean, you think your grandparents have a reason to dislike the moocher. Are you asking me what you should do— then you have to ask a question with the voice up high at the end— or are you just saying, 'I think they have a strong case against this fellow'?"

"Strong case against."

"Well, you may be right, lambikins. You may be correct. Not too many men in this day and age are worth losing your true family for. Now, your true family comes to you through time and space with deep longing, looking only for you, the real you. That I can tell you."

Monica and I eyed each other. Later we would talk.

"Not too crazy, yeah?"

"Ony *li-li*, some time."

Every chance we had, we would bring her mangoes, or somebody's extra jelly or maybe a flower, even some anthuriums that popped out of her own long forgotten greenhouse. Visiting her was like seeing new places and hearing strange ideas. When she got mad at some news about MacArthur, she flared her nostrils. I had seen a picture of a wild horse snorting in a picture book at the library. Mrs. W. had the same strongly drawn lines about her. She volunteered opinions and discussed the news as much as our mothers discussed each other. Jeannie Joanne was mentioned only in passing every once in a while. Monica and I would exchange looks or tap each other's leg under the table when she got started.

"Now, Jeannie Joanne would have enjoyed seeing *The Easter Parade*, don't you think? The blessed child had eyes as big as Judy Garland's."

Monica and I did not humor her.

We could help her all we wanted, but it looked like she would never quit. She liked her loneliness. She couldn't help it. On top of her craziness, she was a *haole*. A double whammy. That meant she was convinced that she could always have her way. No matter what. Something about the law. Our parents talked about examples using *haoles* a lot.

Thinking some about how different *haoles* were from us, I worried about how Mrs. W. was going to get along. For one thing they all looked alike. But dressing like a man, Mrs. W. was too weird and, talking to herself, too old to fit in. And something in an old *haole* lady's face said sad things. In Kohala I had seen an aged turtle which had been speared then dragged onto shore by a fisherman. Its face was deeply wrinkled and, the only witness, I saw a tear run out of its disappointed eye. When the eye caught me staring, it looked as if it recognized me and pleaded with me to let it go. Mrs. Withamm, such a lady and so fierce, reminded me of the beached turtle. Whatever it tried to say to other creatures, it could not speak words about the hurt which showed itself naked under the flat sun.

Wrinkled and fragile, layers of innermost self protruded when Mrs. W. didn't plan to show herself. Sometimes her eyes, like peepholes, gave her away. Often it was how she said something. "Jeannie Joanne is no longer with me. She wasn't meant to be." Or how she stared with longing at us, patted our heads or stroked our backs and then rushed us away from her. Then a wise eye, seeming worldly-wise and all mother, watched us scamper away.

We always came back again.

We sat meekly at her table. Monica's round, smooth face watched her every move with interest. I heard her words on and off. I liked the piles of magazines, every *Life* ever mailed, and her shiny records. Knowing how Monica liked to draw, Mrs. W. showed her photos of Picasso in the magazines and teased her "Miss Monica Picasso" when she brought in a drawing. She even hung them on the walls so we could see them. She admired them out loud, which made Monica twist happily in her seat.

I decided then and there to draw, too, and copied everything Monica did thereafter down to the signature. For the first time I wrote "Lei" on my paper. The surprise was that Monica let me, so I knew she must think of me as her best friend, after all. Being in Mrs. W.'s made a difference.

Mrs. W. had stacked 78s on each other in black piles and the jacket covers by themselves. When she played them for us on her battered player with its raspy needle, the rich music rippled out like a tide of foreign language. We listened quietly. We knew it was supposed to be good for us.

Her fun was crazy. She wanted to be able to hear me or Monica say something like Khachaturian or Mussorgsky or Sibelius. When we did it right, she laughed a lot and said, "Ah, good," all the wrinkles shaking together.

I wondered idly what you would have to do to get such fierce wrinkles. O-Baban, almost ninety, didn't seem to have so many of them. Did you have to be *haole* to shrivel so much? Would half of me shrivel while the other half stayed tight? Would I wrinkle from head to waist or feet to waist? Or would it be the right half or the left half? They said I was *hapa*. Which half would turn *haole?* Where she wasn't shriveled, she was red from scratching. She worried aloud about her nervous itching.

"You see, I have to wear these men's garments to protect my arms. These rashes appear and disappear but never completely."

She rolled up the long *palaka* sleeves to show us the red irritation at her arm creases.

"Oooh . . . must be so-wa, yeah?"

"No, not really. But it feels like a creeping fire under my skin. The sun's always been too hot for me."

She had Monica and me pick aloe leaves, thick with sticky sap, hidden in a corner of her faded garden, to relieve her itch.

From my sizing her up, I saw her arms at least weren't as weak with softening age as her wobbly neck was. My Baban had that kind of pillow flesh. I remembered how much I liked to nestle against grandma's soft arms and burrow myself into her cool protection. I grew sadder with the memory, knowing she was so far away. She had told me not to worry about the dying turtle, that it knew I was not the one who harmed it, that it was family, a guardian of her whole family; she called it *aumakua.*

When I told Mrs. W. about the turtle guide and Baban's soft arms, Mrs. W. only laughed and said nothing. When she was happy, when she laughed from deep inside, all her wrinkles ran away. I could imagine the other her, the one that used to go around and do things out in the open daylight, playing proudly with her kids outside the big house.

But her mood would change just as quickly and though we were certain she meant us no harm, she would snarl in real or mock anger, "Now, the two of you get on home, out, out!" We would be disappointed about not having learned anything again. We wanted to know about the baby. What did happen to dear little

Jeannie Joanne? Could she be the lady who drove over to check on Mrs. W. every once in a while? She wasn't too old; maybe Jeannie Joanne was still alive. Even though we knew for sure the juicy stuff was not what we were getting, we kept coming back for more.

The funny thing that morning was we knew something was up. We ate our baloney sandwiches as we roller-skated down her driveway, around and around the pond. We talked about the new big Piggly Wiggly Supermarket where Monica's mother was hired part-time. She gave us the oil paper package which was printed in yellow with the lettering: b-o-l-o-g-n-a, which made no sense but looked better to eat than the rough slabs Makiki Market would hack out of their meat case. Everyone in Makiki Court would be at the grand opening morning for the samples and the party. Some already waited in the parking lot as we would also, but we needed to find Mrs. W. We wanted her there because she told us that she had "never had a chance to hear real Hawaiian music of that faded era." She could have that; she would probably save the flyer we brought her and later the balloon she would get. We had a lot to tell her. A troupe of hula dancers would be there. We had saved her the red casing strips from the baloney, four of them, long and spidery, very new.

But first we had to skate around, eating nervously because we could hear her crying inside. She made noise in her sorrow; she was angry in her misery. She even wailed aloud. No shame. *Haoles* were like that. She let the world know she was being dumped upon by a miserable man. We knew the story, this was a new tune.

"The old goat, the old goat!" Her screaming it out punctuated our gulps of breakfast and we moved out, up the driveway, ready to leave, as we skated deliberately, back and forth.

Except Monica had a glass knee. She fell again. It was always her left leg. She would fall every time. It didn't have to be because of roller-skating. She could jam up running, skipping, jumping rope. I once watched her fall when she walked toward me. I think it was Mrs. W.'s shrieks of misery which startled us as Monica and I raced to see who could finish the crust part first that made her fall.

As usual the knee was a bloody mess and Monica yelped in little yipping barks. Then she howled in true all-out agony when I touched it a little. I felt bad for having raced her. I made her sit on the grass and tried to open a rusty faucet.

"Owweee . . . ."

When I returned to Monica, there was Mrs. W. examining her leg and not even yelling or crying anymore.

"Oh good," she was saying. It meant nothing. Only her puffed eyes showed us the face of her earlier weeping.

Was she happy my friend got hurt? I cocked my head in her direction to hear more. She was talking to the leg as far as I could tell. In a confidential way. And Monica was very quiet.

Just like my Baban's friend, the old Prayer Lady, Mrs. W. stared at the hurt place. Whenever she came to our house to help cure Baban's aches, the Prayer Lady looked deeply into the exact place where the pain came from. When the old lady prayed it sounded like, "NNNNNnnnnnnnng . . . ." And she liked to touch your head, maybe to see if you were still awake. If you were sleeping she might start to burn some *yaito* directly onto your naked skin, and you wouldn't even jump until you smelled the burning punk. I liked to squish the heaps of tiny ashes on Baban's fleshy back. Soft gray old. Silky. And Baban always got well.

When Mrs. W. talked into Monica's knee, she looked as tense as Baban's friend did, and I relaxed. She didn't do any "nnnnnnnng," but her lips moved as if she were praying silently. Her hand was held over the wound in that healing way I remembered. I wondered if she would hold Monica in her arms and if . . . Monica would die . . . I wasn't worried. I was waiting.

The red stain stopped growing and Monica patted it very slowly with spit on her pocket hankie, the one that held a quarter and a dime tightly knotted in the other corner. The dark red part on her knee looked like a shiny mountain apple of soreness and the roughness of the abrasion on her smooth skin made me wince. She saw my queasy open mouth.

"Hey, Lei, 'as okay!"

We both laughed. Mrs. W. looked up and the light was in her eyes. She stopped mumbling.

"You girls can come on back here later on."

Good try though it was, we were in for the duration.

"W'at fo' you was crying loud, Mrs. W.?"

She sat down hard next to us.

"Oh. Oh. I guess you might as well hear it all from me. I could strangle that old goat. He's sold the property from right under me."

"Owweee . . . " Monica hit the edge of the sore against a chinaberry branch. The two of them were crying together when I finally got the faucet to turn. After the red rusty water, a trickle of clear water flowed out.

"Turn that damn thing off!"

I found myself looking at the old goat.

His face red with anger, his eyes disgusted with me for something I did all wrong, his mouth moving into words I would not like, Mr. Withamm looked down at me. She saw it all quickly.

They stood up solidly against each other. Neither one would allow the other the right to pass. As they yelled into each other's faces, their bodies twisted and moved slowly by degrees until they were practically touching. I cleared out and hid with

Monica. Between the man and the woman so much ill feeling existed that they acted like two magnets repelling each other. Any accidental or intentional contact would defile them both. Faces crazy with pain, they yelled on instead of talking, as if it were natural, the only way to face the other.

Their argument at full speed, they both talked at once, each claiming deadly injury caused by the other. Monica and I tried to make out the words but they filled our ears in reckless fury. The gesture of rage, Mr. W.'s hammering one hand with the other, took my full attention. I noticed he didn't actually hit her, not like the other fathers. We knew how the men picked on the women; it was nothing so different, except that these *haole* people built it up so long with the talking. Usually talking calmed down the mothers we knew.

Mrs. W. grew hysterical, anyway.

"You tried to kill me. You forced me into the hospital. Every way you tried backfired on you and still you persist. You want to squeeze the life out of me with lawyers. Don't you know you will never be able to get rid of me?"

"You crazy woman. You embarrass me! Not even the asylum could hold you down. Listen carefully. I will build a first-class high-rise here and nothing you do can stop me. No tricks of yours can delay me now. You have never been able to do anything but spend my money. You're plain disgusting, Jean. Look at you."

He backed off, holding a finger to his nose as if he smelled something stink.

Mrs. W. let loose.

"I curse you. May every action you take against me spite you. May you be struck down by the hand of almighty God. May you die in agony and regret your dirty life."

Mrs. W. spat on his shoe.

Monica and I cowered.

This felt worse than watching the father and the mother take swings at each other. We were well hidden by the back steps, but I grew nervous with the same old feeling: *Maybe one is gonna kill the other one. For real. And us next.*

Mrs. W. continued to curse him as he made his getaway, until his white car, jerking backwards up the driveway, screeched and caromed into the street. She pointed a finger at his enraged face and yelled out a stream of the same words, "Curse you, curse you, curse you." Her stink eye was wilder than anyone's. He just couldn't stare her down and drive backwards. His face got redder and his hair whiter.

She won that round.

But when he was out of sight, she sighed hard and crumpled.

We got her propped up, sat her in the shade against the house. We wiped her forehead with our hands wet from her tap. She smiled tight for us, and she didn't look like an old man at all. She held each of our damp hands and wept for a while longer. When she was okay, she sent us home.

I said to Monica, "Who's Jean?"

"That's her, 'Jeannie Joanne.'"

"Oh yeah." I knew that. *Turtle.*

Two days later we saw "da ol' fut" as Mama called Mr. Withamm. He drove along the street very slowly in his white Oldsmobile, two careful hands gravely steering the car. He looked just like any regular old *haole* man with white hair and glasses, but we knew what he could be. I couldn't imagine him being a regular father. At least he didn't pretend smile. He sized up the old house, then looked sharply at us, our heads together while we squatted on the front patch of grass. He didn't suspect we were keeping guard.

We did not eye him back, but as soon as the car passed by, we stared at its back end, wishing him a swift accident. Monica said a bad word in Ilocano, starting with p, which I tried hard to memorize as I couldn't ask her to repeat it. She motioned me not to speak.

Relieved that he was gone, we hurried to Mrs. W's window with our report, "Oh, he uuujiii ugly, dat mean one."

Mrs. W. was too busy. She nodded her head. She heard. She was packing a suitcase. Mrs. Withamm planned to leave Hawai'i. We couldn't believe the words we heard.

"I have to go soon. My family will take me in, thank goodness."

"You cannot let him shove you around l'dat."

"My daughter has a farm in Vermont. She will let me stay with her forever. She has a barn that will hold all my worldly possessions quite adequately."

"Jeannie Joanne?" I asked.

"My daughter, the youngest. Muriel."

"But how come you wen' tell all kine story about da bebe l'dat?"

"She is my namesake."

Mrs. W. seemed so sensible in her answer and her directions to us that we helped her pack her clothing willingly. I had to ask her my question before we left her.

"W'atchoo gon' do wid all da stuff?"

"Lamb pie, you are not to worry. Everything's been planned for a long, long time. When you have inner resources and true family, you can do things people would never think of."

Mrs. W. surprised us then with what we had never thought of. She had brought two piles into the living room, waved at them and pointed to each of us.

My pile was the gift of July, 1953.

Monica's pile was the funnies, a whole summer's worth.

All the daily newspapers of an entire month were col-lected and neatly tied up into a bundle several inches thick. I was confused. I whispered to Monica.

"W'at fo' I gon' take 'em home? Mo' betta she keep 'em ova hea and den she get everything jes' how she like 'em. Notting missing, yeah?"

Monica wasn't sure she wanted her weathered cigar box either.

The old old smell again. Roughly cutout, frayed paper pictures of little *haole* girls in smocked dresses, holding pet rabbits and little dogs, standing under Christmas trees, wearing lacy party clothes, riding ponies, acting in plays, dancing as balleri-nas, eating cookies, dressing like Shirley Temple long ago in curly ringlet wigs, opened our eyes wide. We had paper dolls. These things were thin faded newspaper and magazine photos. What could we do with them?

Mrs. W. was so happy to give her collections to us. She smiled and waited lovingly when she pressed her presents into our hands. Our eyes met tenderly.

But we kept our mouths shut. Not for nothing had we been trained so well. Our mothers made us practice saying thank you and showing gratitude more than once. O-Baban even held my head down just so to get the bow timing right in case old Japanese people came over. They never came in without handing something over. The idea was to beat it fast, so you wouldn't have to say too much or act too cute.

"Okay. Thenks, Mrs. W., yeah?" A big smile.

"Thenk you so much. You always soo nice. We going go now."

Monica left the cigar box on top of the pile which we placed very carefully under my house. We cleared a place on the dirt, spread out an old plastic raincoat and made sure the pile was far in enough from the wooden slats so that the newspapers wouldn't get wet or be seen. After all, we never heard of anybody at all getting anything from Mrs. W.

We would disappear under the house to hide our secrets. Mine was the last one in the back row of Makiki Court homes, old plantation houses moved away from the cane fields and herded together closely around the only other house on our street which was a big as Mrs. W.'s. It was crisscrossed by added walls and extra doors to make it into seven apartments, and it wasn't right in the line of nosy mothers' sight.

A tiny green door, its hasp locked with a long nail, led to the crawl space. Our fingers stretched to shut it tight from inside. Monica and I first tried out cigarettes and one of Duffy's girly magazines there by the light from that opening. In the cool dirt we found privacy. We feared only centipedes and getting caught. If we were seen we would be forever blamed for any old house fire caused by kids "playing matches" in any direction near us. We planned on not getting caught.

We didn't bother our paper piles until the day Mrs. W. left for the mainland. We sat in the front row of neighbors perched on the sloping hill of grass across the street from her house, waiting to see what was up. It was because the Matson vans and the big trailers kept pulling up that the whole neighborhood turned out.

Carpenters had been working long days on what they finally achieved. The entire front of the big house, cut up into chunk sections like a puzzle, was ready to be stuffed into the arriving vans. You could see right into Jeannie Joanne's light blue bedroom. All the furniture had been packed up and shipped off.

The cross section of the house let us see all the rooms at once. It was a big spread. And there was no master bedroom, she was right.

Mrs. W. walked around her rooms directing workmen here and there, not noticing all the people across the street. Not focusing on us at all, though we talked and moved around. Funny as the circus of workmen looked, sawing and hauling, splitting wooden beams and kicking walls as they scurried through the rooms and tried to fit whole sections into the sea vans, Mr. W. was funnier. No sooner did we spot the white car, then it disappeared again. He kept driving around the block to see what was going on. His red face grew angrier each time. You could tell he was burning up because the whole noisy show was out of his control.

Auntie Annabelle said, "Eh, look the buggah. No mo' dog to bodda him, now he gon' turn in da wife!" Nobody liked him, so they all laughed at him. She was right, he was the one who called the Humane Society anytime he saw a dog on the street, even the pet dogs with collars.

Mrs. W. kept two workmen busy loading up one of the vans with her piles of rubbish. They weren't happy about loading stacks and stacks of old trash into the sea vans, but she persisted, talked all the time, and the rubbish was beginning to line up for the move. She knew how to give orders and command attention. Her children, the nervous *haole* man and the lady with a hat, waited helplessly on the lanai steps. They, too, did not see us. But you could tell they didn't want to.

Mrs. W. looked like she had dressed up. She wore a crisp, white shirt, sleeves rolled up, over her baggy pants. I thought I saw some lipstick on her and pointed it out to Monica. Monica held her finger to her lips as a warning and pointed out what was coming.

Mr. Wittham was trying to pay the foreman to stop work. He argued, red faced, and pulled out a roll of money as he gestured to say his wife was crazy. She couldn't see what he was doing. She continued to scold a workman because the rubbish pile was stuck in a standstill.

We braced ourselves for the big fight. Mrs. W. moved toward the old fut like a cat with its hair standing up, when she figured out why the work stopped.

At first they talked too softly for anyone to hear. When they yelled, the electricity in their anger came out flashing. This time they went for each other in front of all the neighbors. Their children, who were as old as mothers and fathers themselves, came running and held on to their mother. The foreman held Mr. Wittham's hands behind his back.

She said it again. Mrs. W. turned to all of us watching and screamed what we knew she would.

"I curse him to death. He's going to die soon. Wait and see."

Some ladies cried out in shock, and Auntie Annabelle clapped. We all looked at the unsmiling old *haole*. He just got angrier and went away in his white car. Their children put her in their car and drove her off too. She didn't see us at all. But nobody else went away. The carpenters kept their work going, and we all watched as if the stuff was ours. They packed it all, all the piles and all the front of the house. The back section was left for bulldozers later.

Slowly moving back to the Court, the neighbors talked about *haoles*. As for us, we were heavy with what we had seen.

We sat under our house, looking at each other and Mrs. W.'s gift. We moved carefully to examine the pile of papers, so as not to stir up too much dust.

Monica sneezed.

She went through the cutout girls. I thumbed over the newspapers, reading at random. I saw the Piggly Wiggly grand opening ad and noticed the part about a band, "special appearance." Wondering why nobody said anything about it, I thought about how we missed the dancing.

We heard a familiar voice. Monica's mother was searching the street for her and had stopped to yell at our front door.

"Mon-i-ca! Moneecca! Mon-i-ca! You gon' get it! Confunnit!"

She stormed back in the other direction as her voice grew softer and smaller.

"Oh oh. She mad. Must be my brudda ate somet'ing again."

We waited cautiously before Monica squat-waddled out and ran home. I wondered if she was right. Did Boy eat the chili peppers we told him were *menehune* dingalings? The buggah loved attention.

I was alone.

Under the house felt lonely, but I was tired and I dozed. The sound of drops of water plunking on the border of *ti* plants growing in a line under the eaves of the house woke me up. All the people's faces, activities, events, ads and symbols of what our world was all about in those newspapers floated through my mind. They meant little to me. I didn't need to hold on to whatever Mrs. W. found so precious. *Old nuspepa.*

I had only been curious in leafing through the messy pages. I had piled them neatly back into an upside-down stack. They were a whole month old and just useless junk. My decision came back to the feeling that they were boring but possibly useful for sitting on, especially on rainy days. Or maybe Monica and I could find a 55-gallon drum and make a real fire at the dump. She knew how to get wooden matches.

I kicked the stack of papers a little further away from me and noticed that the last one ran an ad for beachfront home lots for sale. And in the photo, there next to a wall map, stood my real father. It was the guy. *Haole.* The one Mama was talking to when we went to the tax office.

I studied the hand pointing at the map, took in the pattern of the plaid shirt he wore. The map, the shoes, the pointer stick took my careful, patient attention.

Listening to the raindrops, I looked and looked at the face.

W hen I woke up in the morning light the word returned to my mind. Disown, dis-own. Disown carried such a sad ooh sound.

The night before, Mama had been telling the neighbor, Mrs. Ajifu, about her life and how she had left the Big Island for good. I took notice when Mama said, "And den my fada w'en disown me." I had gotten stuck at the word disown which circled back on itself. How could O-Jiji have disowned her, unless he had owned her all along? Getting to the reason O-Jiji threw her out, which had been her pregnancy with me, Mama had been angrier than I had ever seen her. Too intent on pretending not to have heard, I had stopped short of asking for more informa-tion. I would have to time my questions for when she wasn't so angry or rushed, because she always had to go to work.

THE CURSE CLOSET

Until then, time had no special meaning for me. I had been content not to worry about what had happened before and what would be-come of us. But since I had turned twelve, I was concerned about why we were different from the other families and why I wasn't like girls my age, which was an entirely different thing. Although the clues were everywhere, I was unsure how to look them over. The heavy word *disown*, which had made Mama turn her face to the floor with clenched teeth, said something about my grandparents and their being Japanese, which also meant a veil of shame cover-ing something I had tried and tried to figure out. Mrs. Ajifu had softly stroked Mama's back, but there had been nothing I could do.

I lay on the metal bed I shared with my grandma, thinking. In the cluttered bedroom of the Makiki Court frame house, I could be myself, all alone, in only one place. A small door blended into the wall. Almost hidden by a heaped dresser whose mirror shone out into the early morning light, the closet behind it showed only its outlines where the hideaway door fit into the wall. The closet had always been a crowded space filled with sharp-edged boxes and random, lumped shapes.

All there was left of the Kohala days was stored in there. Out of a metal tube canister, a tightly rolled sepia photo unfurled longer than my arms stretched out wide and told of O-Jiji's impressive funeral. Everyone had said his death was a shock because he had been upright and unbowed, strong to the very end. He was defeated by sudden stroke and a violent heart attack which took him down. The thunderbolt news of his death had sent Mama and me back to Kapa'au where we became mourners.

In the funeral photograph I was the small head in the middle next to the coffin and O-Baban. Enormous floral arrangements on stick legs were propped to our side. My mother stood with her sisters on the end away from the one brother still in the islands after the war. The rigid faces of the old people, sad and formal in their temple clothes, and most of the Nakamura clan, solemn and together in one place for the last time, spread out across that still portrait. It was the photo they would send to O-Jiji"s home village in Hiroshima where family and the few old friends of his youth might sit in wonder to see all the people, he, that poor farmer, a solitary dreamer, had somehow engendered or befriended. They would register surprise at my grandmother's sorrow-lined face, saying, "How old she looks. Didn't she used to be from around here; doesn't she still have brothers in the district; aren't all those overseas people supposed to be wealthy?"

O-Baban had had an angry falling out with Uncle Johnny, her most prominent son, over the sale of the little Kapa'au house. Uncle handled all the money because he was the oldest as well as being the broker for the sale. There had been nothing left to give her anyway, he claimed, saying he had used the profits to pay for the elaborate funeral demanded by O-Jiji's position in the community. Uncle Johnny was probably right, but his mother wouldn't agree and refused to speak to him. He reminded his sisters, who either took his side or looked knowingly at him, that the women had asked for the big funeral. Denying any responsibility, he claimed females had no right to grumble about details. As I heard it, eventually they realized he had the final say, but my mother and grandmother turned their faces away from him and whispered about the expensive home he had built in Honolulu.

My mother's two other brothers were in Japan, one an unrepentant concentration camp returnee who said to America, "Ship me back to a Japan I've never known, then, if my World War I medals and my school teaching years count for nothing about my character and loyalty," and the other, a complaisant member of the Occupation Forces in Tokyo, who normally said nothing to anyone. The sisters didn't count in the matter of inherited property, because they were all married and belonged now to other families, even my mother, no longer a Nakamura.

Mama and I got O-Baban, O-Jiji's name seal, their original Japanese government passports to Hawai'i, and plantation contracts dated in the 1890s. His ashes in an urn came with her. Her Buddhist altar arrived in a crate. They had been married over sixty years, and she had been younger than he by fifteen years, although they looked equally old to me.

In her boxes were packed some mysterious packages she called unimportant things which gave me a deep curiosity about their real worth. I knew she would not have been so careful to understate their importance otherwise. Out of one bundle came a heavily embroidered silk tiger tapestry which turned out to be a *sumo-tori*'s fringed ceremonial skirt. A shade of golden red thread, shimmering in a metallic way, gave the animal's eyes a wild defiance. In its plain energy the tiger reminded me of my mother, since O-Baban told me long ago that Mama had been born in Tiger Year. When I asked O-Baban how she got the tapestry, she hesitated. She said one of the temple ladies had begged her to hold it for her husband who was being cursed by people who said he flaunted his prowess as an amateur *sumo* wrestler. He himself had been asked to hold on to the regalia, to keep it in safekeeping for its original owner. Or O-Baban may have hidden it for the family directly after the Japanese attacked Pearl Harbor and federal authorities made the rounds, checking the homes of "suspect" Japanese for evidence that they were more Japanese than the other 160,000 Japanese in Hawai'i. O-Baban had never in her life trusted government agents of any country so she would have been the perfect old lady to hold on to something everyone agreed was dangerous. The apron was meant to signify the fighter's name as well as to protect his manly parts from harmful stares.

O-Baban kept these objects wrapped in neatly tied squares of *furoshiki* cloth and stowed them away from sight so that I knew for sure that they had their own importance and right to some private space. That privacy was what I was growing to need more and more.

For years Mama had told me that someday I would get "it." She described how she found out what it felt like as she pressed the long sleeve of one of her brother's white shirts with a charcoal-burning iron. She burned it in panic while she suddenly felt a strange trickle running down her leg and thought that she was bleeding to death. In order to help me avoid any similar confusion, Mama was going to set me straight early on what women had to go through when they got the curse. The alternate words like *term*, *rags*, *on her moon*, and *my friend* intrigued me. I listened very politely. After all, had I not sat through the sixth grade lecture for-girls-only in a darkened cafeteria to watch the Kotex film which started with a flower and ended up in diagrams of reproductive organs in an invisible woman? Enduring the movie while I sat next to popular girls, like Patricia Pang, who didn't even want me in her gang, made me realize I was just tolerated, because I wasn't yet mature. Unlike Patricia, who was the kind of girl I wanted to be, I didn't have my period yet. Patricia fit right in, did all the things teachers expected and every adult admired. She wore a pink polka-dotted swing skirt with a poodle appliqued on it. She got her mother to sew up book bags with appliqued initials for all the members of her club. I heard Monica, my onetime buddy, describe her with a longing smile, "That Patricia, she's so petite." All the powerful P words were hers: polite, pretty, and most of all, popular. Of course she was the first to have her period. Even her hair held a successful wave, permanently.

Having given up on trying to look like everybody else, since I was taller, bigger and so washed out in color, I decided to turn myself into "Miss Personality Plus." I told myself I was much better in choral singing than Patricia, who claimed she knew all the words to the Top 40 songs on the radio. Not only that, I was one of the females who knew exactly what to expect from menstruation and had even received a sample sanitary pad from the company through the nurse's office. I wanted to tell my mother, "I'm cued in, Mama!" but my tiger mom probably wouldn't have been impressed, anyway.

I thought about the other important thing Patricia did. She used her full name at every opportunity.

"No, no, you gotta call me Patricia. Not Pat or Patty. Never have been. My full name is Patricia P. K. Pang." I remembered the way she expected compliance and corrected everyone who didn't call her Patricia.

I tried it out aloud in bed, "No, please call me Leiko Lorraine. Not just Lei." But it was hopeless. Lei was familiar and easy to hear. But what if I had a real with-it name, a *haole* name like Margo Whittier, which came to me as suddenly as the closet light would go on when the cord was pulled. Margo Whittier was like Barbie but with a last name that counted. Somehow the surname Duffland didn't have the power I definitely needed. Leiko Duffland had no class to it. The first name didn't match. Margo Whittier was so smooth and electric with its whoosh of air and tapping t's. When I pretended to be Margo Whittier in a polka dot dress, not a pink one, and said, "Nah, Lei . . . mo' bettah," I opened my eyes to the bright bedroom, happy, sort of.

I spied a heap of folded clothing reaching up from the floor at the foot of the bed. It was clear to me that my mother wanted me to waste my days slaving over those endless clothes. She was like that. She left it to me to figure out what she wanted me to do. I had to anticipate what she required or get endless scoldings for what was undone and what she viewed as my total laziness. She always set up work for me before she left for work, which reminded me that she was working for me. Her regular lecture about being the only breadwinner for the family now that Duffy had ditched us didn't bother me. I had watched him return every so often, more or less sober, and had seen Mama walk around with a distant expression as if she had tasted something very strong which left her wondering about how to clean her mouth. But even if Duffy left for good, I wouldn't think about it overmuch. I had to iron.

Mama had left the ironing board lying across my path out to the door. She even left the door to the closet wide open, the dresser moved aside. She had cleared out all the old boxes and clutter, but the *furoshiki*-wrapped things were still on the top shelf in neat order. Under them I saw the row of metal hangers like ugly teeth in a cavernous mouth, waiting to be filled.

When I approached the board, I caught a glimpse of my face in the dresser drawer mirror. At least my longer hair gave me the look of a real girl now, I reassured myself, ignoring the paleness of the *hapa* face which stared back in ill humor.

Soon one piece of ironing after another occupied my hands. Not even "Que Sera, Sera," bleating out of the radio or random thoughts of being invited to Patricia's birthday party at the Waikiki Theater could take me out of gloom. The ironing stretched out and would probably fill up the day.

The warm trickle running down my leg as I ironed my khaki JPO skirt with the electric iron and listened to the latest pop songs was a wet surprise. Somehow foresight came to me. I unplugged the iron, propped it up, clicked off the radio and then rushed to the bathroom to examine the miraculous blood produced on my own without anyone's demanding it. I had no brother to beat me up because of a burned shirt, no sisters to make fun of my sissy fear and no mother who would hand me a bunch of old rags to stuff into my underpants. I had a booklet and a sanitary belt and pad. I had read it many times and arranged the equipment over and over. But when I finally wore it, the padding stuck out awkwardly, and I could barely walk. Whether I was proud of being a woman or sad about being different yet again was fuzzy in my mind. The morning, as I felt it, which had started out badly, was changing rapidly.

When I realized what the blood meant, I felt for the first time the small ache at my center and the tiny shiver of cold moving up my spine. Alternating with numbness came more feeling, a jolt of it, than I had ever remembered experiencing down there. Worries flooded through me, *Will I get pregnant right away now? I am only a child, will I be carrying a child?* A wave of crazy laughter welled up within me at that disturbing thought. I knew better, but this part wasn't in the movie: the coldness inside, then the heat and my eyes welling up with tears when the tingling started again. I didn't want to change at all. It wasn't fair.

In the bathroom I stared at the blood with interest: just a bit and dark red. *That kind of pain for so little? Will more come and make me sick?* The evidence of my new maturity, my stained panties lay on the counter before me. This spot, deep and dark in color was thrilling, but scary. I began to wonder why I needed such a thick layer of protection. *Will I begin to bleed until the Kotex pad gets soaked through? Should I get out another from Mama's big box?* As I examined the belt holding the large white wad of padding by hooks, I looked with interest at my naked lower body. A light haze of brownish pubic hair, something I tried to forget I had recently grown, greeted my eyes. Still no *chichis*.

I felt a twinge of pain in my abdomen, clutched it, stricken, and moved back against the wall for support. I had interpreted it to be the first of wrenching pains. There would be waves of sore stomach for sure. Nothing happened.

I pulled on my jeans and buttoned up my shirt.

I saw that the mirror looked back at me, the shiny girl with new hair. Clear as light, it let me know that change had finally come.

Washing my panties took my concentrated attention. I sniffed the spot of blood: a tang of sea combined with unmistakable humanness hit my nose. I touched the dark colored blood spot, it was slightly slippery and its shine felt cool to my fingertips. My grandmother had called women's blood *gei-gei*, and her distaste for the word made me worried as I touched what must surely have been very dirty. She had told me grown women were always the last to bathe in the *furo* tub because they were unclean. Scrubbing the blood with soap and water helped dilute the deep color, but blood was tough. A brown stain remained on the underpants no matter how much I scrubbed and squeezed. Just like the Japanese flag, there was that circle of color in the middle of the white material. I would let it stay. I would hang the panties on the line and see if anyone noticed anything at all. I wondered if they would consider my blood any different from my mother's, if they would say anything to me. Probably not. But I felt different anyway.

Quietly I worked my way through the empty house back to the hateful iron. I looked around at the room, ordinary, sunlit and quiet. My eyes fell upon the open closet. Noiselessly I went in and closed the door behind me. In the corner O-Baban also stored our extra rice in a fat hundred-pound-sized bag. I felt as if I had not eaten for years. The flesh of my body was tight, hard and tired. I would dry up into a dead hibiscus, then a crumbled leaf, then bits of trampled, brittle leaf bits, then a bright smear like the trail of a snail, glittering in the light, but only a leftover, a residue on the path. I would be gone and then free. It was the body talking, aching and slowly falling apart, the first of all the signs. Frozen by this first time, I sensed the final leaving. I sat on the bag of rice feeling out the best place to sit so that the hump of padding would settle in just so, and I wouldn't fall off. But I was already at the edge of something which made me shift my weight on the rice bag to catch myself in time.

The darkness in the closet was silent and comforting, lulling me wide-eyed into a place where I could get sad and not have to explain. Steadily, I drifted deeper; I watched myself as the child who happily played games, skipped rope, and hopped around in a circle without ever having to stop. I was getting into a kind of paralysis, solidifying imperceptibly. The rice bag smell, chaff dust and powdered grains, comforted me and reminded me of all the plantation houses in a row. The one my mother grew up in, the familiar full no-smell smell of rice cooking, of rice bag material airing on the porch, the sounds of children playing, blurring together, and the new quieter me I had become from inside out.

Who am I, am I? the little voice asked me. The "Que Sera" tune. Only the words turned into a worrisome question which repeated in a pattern that I allowed to blur like the sounds of children playing long ago in the dusty red dirt garden. If someone should see me frozen, I reasoned, I would stay very quiet and unmoving so that no one could see me apart from things or plants, no one could break me away from this being part of everything not human. Then no one would see me or bother me at all again ever. I could be the clouds above or breathe myself into the trees or become part of the grassy ground, invisible, but still existing everywhere. I would be a house, sleeping, eyes the windows and mouth the door. Frozen meant something rigid as a blade, like the trickle of cold feeling in my stomach, like the tightness of my spine forced into a new hard posture. When once I was soft and dough-y like the sweet *chi-chi dango* O-Baban liked to make, now I was made of hard rice granules, left forgotten. I hummed a tune from a radio memory but the song buzzed off into silent notes.

From inside the dark closet, I was aware of the nebulous light shifting outside, evidence of which showed through the cracks where the door was outlined. The shape of a door in light. This was the closet where Duffy once stored a stack of girly magazines. It didn't matter. This was where O-Baban hid the tiger tapestry above the big bag of rice. It wasn't forbidden any more. This was where I would hide out to think about what was outside. Now that I had become female and bloody, I had crossed over to something. All I had to do was figure out what the something was.

I sat breathing in the sense of harmony that came from sleeping in the bright darkness which filled me with energy. The secret urgency of hiding melted away, and I floated in a trance between worlds. O-Baban and O-Jiji were both young. I became my mother, Katie.

She and I were one. She lived in Japanese camp and she had to iron everyday. She hated ironing for her older brothers, because they bossed her over it. The long white shirts needed so much starch to keep them firm enough to prop her brothers' necks up stiffly. Up and up. The word *oppa* came back. I saw little girls in a row, each carrying another child on her back. "Oppa me," the toddlers cried out to be carried. Babysitting for family or helping for small change or small words of praise from neighbors, my mother—like the others—tried to be a good girl. Everyone had her burden to carry or a designated child to mind.

Mama was the youngest so the other little girls saw her as the free one, the lucky girl. At the same time they resented the freedom she flaunted and tried to make sure she was aware of their annoyance. Every girl was proudly AJA, American of Japanese Ancestry, but their Japaneseness came first even though their names were clearly English. Mabel, Thelma, Hilda, Daisy and Ethel were Katie's playmates, and they were warned daily not to be with children from any other camp, not to talk to anyone not Japanese. They always obeyed, because they knew how to be good AJA girls.

Uncle Johnny was the boy who came first. He was *taisho,* leader of the pack, the one whose goal was to win. He knew how to extract his due allegiance from the others, and he also knew how to get Katie to do his bidding.

To please him in front of his gang of boy buddies, Katie climbed a thin papaya tree because he insisted she should.

"Climb," he demanded and pointed at a twelve-foot stalk no bigger around than a clothesline pole. Tiny green fruit topped the skinny tree. "Go up or I gon' whack yo' legs, den poke yo' *okole,* if you no move!" He waved his bamboo switch in her face.

She nervously eyed him and remembered the last "favor" he had done for her. He said she didn't have to iron his khaki pants after all. He would wear his *saila moku* trousers instead. So she was spared an hour's drudgery. Now he meant to amuse his friends by making his personal monkey perform.

"I no' like," she demurred.

"Go, or else!" He showed her his fist with a samurai mien that made his friends, Ernest and Lester, slap their legs with pleasure.

"Good one, Johnny-boy!"

They enjoyed this new sport. He was good as his word, everyone knew him. Johnny had thrashed Katie more than once before. He had a good uppercut.

Trembling, she began to climb the tiny tree. She shimmied up the tree, that was the plan, two legs tightly astraddle the thicker bottom part, two skinny arms reaching upwards in futility.

Almost immediately, the tree bent forward with a loud creak. "Creeaak . . . ." she dipped down with it, her dirty rice bag pants showing under her faded calico dress.

The boys howled with laughter when the tree crashed at their feet with the heap of girl on top of it. She was the silly fool, more *bakatare* than they had ever seen.

They took off when O-kasan yelled out of her window, "What's going on now? This boy is worse than a devil. Your father will beat you!"

And then O-tosan was there, outrage filling his lean face and his lopsided stance, two legs apart in fury before his stupid offspring. The other boys looked back from where they had scattered. Taking Johnny by surprise O-tosan slapped his face loudly with rough motions and then cuffed him twice to make him remember. Weeping silently, Johnny crouched low. He would get his revenge on her later. There was nothing to say.

Her face turned down to the ground, Katie squatted in front of her father.

"You shame *natta.*" His deep voice used sarcasm as its coiling point.

"*Geddo.* You not my daughter any more. Go way!"

His pronouncement caused steady tears to run down her face. Using her shame to make her obey only him, he spat on the ground. She had been his favorite and the youngest child. Still he purposely insulted her and turned heel on her, saying nothing more, not another word to ease her humiliation.

The row of girls in *chawan* cuts circled Katie, all eyes, all ready to tell the rest of the camp. They moved together, one step nearer to her, and then because she would not appeal to them for anything, because she chose to stare back, they moved a step back. They could spend their lives being good girls, but not my mother, not me. . . . Katie had chosen the way to do it.

She couldn't fight until then. She wouldn't fight until she had lost that battle to her father. Nothing she could say would have helped anyway, and her courage would grow until she learned how to live as a tiger of a woman. She knew this by heart as I would find out for myself in endless ways.

Although she didn't stop crying as she nursed her bruises and dared not look at her father's face, she said in her voice as Mama that she did gain something from that fall. "With a man, you learn the best from a mistake. Never let any guy tell you what to do or how to think."

Floating into place, we girls squatted in a circle. How close we were to the ground then, talking to each other, playing cards or milk covers, eating dripping wet watermelon, spitting away the seeds in the dust. I saw before me the faces of those little girls in rice bag dresses and *chawan*-cut hairdos and the faces of the babies on their backs who wanted only to be held and carried endlessly. The girl who was just a baby was Mama wanting to please, Mama climbing so high on the papaya tree, Mama tumbling down and crying to the sound of laughter when her faded *puka puka* panties showed. She said, "*Oppa* me," and I was not strong enough to pick her up and carry her as she did me.

Picking herself up, she came to help me instead. She squatted and tenderly tied my shoelaces and fixed the rim of my sock. When she stood, she starched my dresses and ironed them, tied a crisp bow at my waist, then quickly braided my hair, one rope after the other. I thought over how it was that she could give me so much of who she was without question and without words. She understood something I could not grasp, and it had to do with this new blood.

The curse, the funeral photo and the tiger skirt encircled me in the closet. I decided I didn't want to be my mother and that she would understand why I wanted to be different, but I couldn't figure out the right steps to take out of her path of suffering. Not that she and I looked alike or thought alike. She was already shorter than my five feet four inches, and I would soon outweigh her as well. I was already the heaviest, tallest and most outspoken of my class, and I felt the difference strongly. My red hair had long changed to brown, but I knew I was marked as odd. Accepted, but totally different. I wanted to change, and now I had changed another way, unexpectedly. I would try being alone, away from groups of girls and what they demanded, whatever they decided all together. No one would own me, and therefore, I could never be disowned.

From my vantage point in the closet I saw Mama, her face masked, not yet who she was to be, in the center of the circle, being watched by all of us. She was not me. I would be different in my own way. I tasted the soft, agreeable unconnectedness which set me aside in peace. Alone, cold, forgotten, I let myself enjoy the quiet self-loathing in my cocoon of secret, dark thoughts.

I was locked into a tiny space and no one knew I was in there. No one cared. No one would ever let me out to talk or move. I was the side of a hill and a wedge of vast space. I was a rock.

The door opened wide. O-Baban faced me in full light.

"Sah!" She was annoyed, but she laughed at me. Her wrinkled face was lively with her invitation.

"Lei-san, come outsai. You, me eat *cha-cha-mumma.*" She used baby words to lure me out to steaming rice and tea with one salty red plum. I abandoned the paralysis. But I noticed that she no longer called me Lei-chan, so I wasn't a baby anymore. She thought I was avoiding the ironing, and she was right.

She fed me and put me to bed. By the end of that first day, I had put the curse away up high on the closet shelf. I was myself again.

*S*he used to be beautiful. Everybody who knew Mama before from the Union Mill camp days said so. The one who told me this repeatedly with a bright-eyed smile was the one I called the Lady. She had been Mama's best friend in school during what they called the olden days.

Whenever she wanted me to look neater or if we were going to see her relatives at a party or a funeral, Mama pulled me along to see the Barber Shop Lady. Was it Mildred? Or Hazel? Maybe Betsy . . . we called her the Lady.

The remains of my *chawan* cut always grew out raggedy, the bangs so fast that I had to brush them out of my eyes when I wanted to see. At least now my hair grew brown, no longer so bright with eye-catching red. Mama was afraid she'd have to buy me glasses. Before long we would head back to the barber shop. Other times my hair was an excuse to visit just to see the Lady and talk story.

FO' W'AT STAY SHAME

We usually started out on a Saturday afternoon as soon as Mama had the rest of the day off. The crowded area of A'ala where the shop was stuck in between a dry cleaner's warehouse and a noodle wholesaler spread out into seedy back alleys. Like the aftermath of a dream, I can't remember exactly how we got there, but I will not forget the feeling of moving around in the Lady's world. Shimmering with heat from the day and bright colors, her block was alive but only partly awake in the daylight. I would spot an occasional foggy breathing heap, a drunken man sleeping off his connection to our sunbaked world. Even the sound of animals yowling, cats fighting, caused no stir in the drunkard's corner.

Several older Filipino males who lived in upstairs rooms settled back to gossip against the dusty brick wall next to her glass-front doorway. They began to look like familiar faces to me as we went there almost every other Saturday. They never bothered us, except for one guy who always spotted her and called out, "Hello, my dahleeng," to my irate mother. Her face went blank as she covered up her feelings. All traces of femininity disappeared, replaced by a no-face face. She preferred to be invisible and never made a sign of having heard him.

Though the street had to be navigated carefully because of the noisy, reeking bars and open traps of tattoo stalls, the Lady's shop was homey and messy. Airy white curtains billowed in the breeze from the small back windows which let in daylight. The outside front sign read Barber Shop with a white and red border.

The doorbell rang with a jingle when we opened the door to her greetings. The Lady bowed formally to us but she gave us a big smile, too. She kept an old photo of Mama and herself Scotch-taped under the glass counter of her display case. Mama's delicate face looked very young and shy then. Her petite frame and eyes looking away from the camera gave an impression of her being eager to leave. The Lady looked right at you from the snapshot, as if pulling you into their picture, like everything was funny and she liked you. They managed to look like they were having fun while wearing complicated kimonos as if it weren't even Hawai'i, but some place in Japan where they might have lived. I stared with amazement that Mama could have been so different then with her frilly permed hair and delicate nostrils.

After a while we were past the waiting for the regular customers to be done. The Lady had brought out all kinds of creams and fade lotions for me to try on my freckles, not that any of them really did the job. My *hapa-haole* skin stayed mottled and my image in the mirror, serious about camouflaging myself. The idea was that I should keep myself busy experimentally rubbing out spots.

Waiting until the two old girlfriends were engrossed in conversation, I liked leafing through boxing, detective and romance magazines, sitting to the side of Mama's line of vision. I checked out the Lady's counters, which were crowded with lavender and white orchid plants. The cupboards, full of tiny drawers, reminded me of O-Jiji's handiwork. I couldn't resist asking who made them for her, remembering all the sawing and pounding and sanding my grandpa did. Mama shushed me when she heard me begin. When she was done with a line of customers, the Lady could think of how she would do me. When the time was right, she looked over at me and nodded to Mama.

While she cut my hair, she kept up a steady conversation, talking story with Mama. Her customers were Filipinos or Japanese, only an occasional *haole* service man found his way in. No one looked twice at us, my mama moving back and forth beyond the far partition to the hotplate to prepare our snack. We never paid her, but we always brought food to eat with her. Sometimes it was as simple as rice, tea and pickles, but the Lady's very favorite was egg rice, *ume* and salty *nori*. My mother deftly cracked the raw eggs into rice bowls, having timed the cooking rice perfectly. The wooden *hashi* made a *tsuru tsuru* slippery sound as Mama beat the *shoyu* egg mixture.

Her tiny beauty spot shifting, the Lady smacked her lips and remembered more camp days when Mama made her familiar food under Baban's heavy, measuring gaze.

When Mama brought up the Lady, she always added "Out of all 'dem, she da one has da appetite." It was high praise. For her friend, Mama searched out the fattest fingers of *lup cheong* and the freshest *daikon kim chee*, the kind with the root still attached to the turnip because the best energy was at that joining point. Selecting a grade of *tofu*, Mama checked for the creamiest, softest looking block, called *kinugoshi* or silk-like, because she knew the Lady could tell instantly what had vitamins and what was stale. The firmer cotton quality, too coarse, didn't pass inspection. The Lady, she said, "knows good stuff, because she know how to eat."

Sometimes they signaled to each other when they saw a woman they didn't like pass in front of the glass window. Mama and the Lady knew how to peer over the little front curtain so that they could see everything without being seen. They were especially incensed by the women they called hula hula girls, only they pronounced it fula-fula and said it with derision.

"Dat kine *wahine* only faking, good fo' nothing. Fool around too much, troublemaker," the Lady would point out to me and Mama in an informational way.

"Da nerve, yeah? All same Hawaiian, dey tell. Not to anybody wid eyes to see. Dey not *Kanaka*, no mo' den you o' me. No mo' shame, dem."

They would alternate, talking in pidgin, then in standard English, sometimes in quick Japanese when they really masked what they said. Mama and the Lady relished any talk about scandals, sitting down together head to head in enjoyment of each other's presence. They repeated how a man named Gouveia, who passed for white through no fault of his own, got into trouble writing bad checks, while pretending to be a *haole* radio announcer named Goodwin; how a Japanese war bride took plenty of poison, but did not die "just down da street, *mauka* side of Dillingham," because her parents sent her a letter asking for more, more money than she could make at her riverside bar; how hard it was to find a decent seamstress at a reasonable price, "no wonda everybody buying from Sears Roebuck Department Store."

The Lady revealed another incident when a wife—she whispered something that sounded like "da one, da husband, da bank no Mista' Murakami"—took it in her head to get "j", meaning jealous. The wife cut the Lady dead as if she saw right through her when they passed each other at the bus stop. The Lady felt she wouldn't even have been recognized if she hadn't been wearing her white seersucker uniform.

"Dat one crazy. Huh. As if I gon' try steal one old *bolo* head man. W'at she take me fo', anyway? Lo-lo, her."

Sometimes there was a surprise. The Lady revealed that she was saving her money to take a trip—her first away from home—to visit the mainland, where her sister lived, but she would go only when her father finally died. She had to wait now, because she felt sorry for him. He had never regained his old self after he had been shipped to relocation camp in Arizona. They whispered the word *camp* then, so different from the way they talked about the regular plantation camps. Mama and the Lady always agreed about the weakness of most men. They shared their disgust about their older brothers. When they talked, it sounded like they had the same brother, the one who got the good education, who never helped with the old parents, who was always right, who reminded everybody that they were obligated to do things for him the way he decided they should be done, who was never wrong even when he lost big, who owned all the family property, and who never gave anything to anyone but his own children.

"W'at fo' we need samurai l'dat, yeah?"

"Yeah. Mo' betta w'en dey wen' make *hara kiri.*"

"Nowadays no mo' *hara kiri* kine. Too bad, yeah?'

When they agreed so much, their heads bobbed up and down for emphasis in recording the correctness of the comments.

The Lady never asked about Duffy, the vague *haole* husband waiting in our house, just as Mama never asked the Lady directly about her plans. As for me, I kept quiet, hoping that they would begin to talk about my real father, but they never let me hear anything important or anything that made them sad. Both knew where the sore spots lay, and they chose to treat them with care. When they turned on the radio, they beamed into soft steel guitar music. To my delight they knew the words to all the *hapa haole* melodies and sometimes even lyrics to the latest pop songs. When it came on, they did *Beyond the Reef* in falsetto with extra vocal flourishes and a vamp here and there, just to amuse us all.

With rolled eyes and screeches of hysterical laughter, they discussed which of the boys from the old Honoka'a Japanese Camp turned *skebbe*.

They agreed some men were just worthless in total. They talked again about the rich *haole* banker and the part-Hawaiian May Day queen with the heart-shaped face whom he would never be able to marry, because his mother wrote a will forbidding him to take a non-*haole* wife. His mother was part-Hawaiian herself, they added in unison and snickered.

"So Lei-chan gotta find yo'self one man who no mo' madda!" the Lady threw this conclusion in my direction.

"No-no-no, Lei gotta get one good education and den one profession and make plenty money." Mama filled with pride when she looked at me and underlined the message with an intent expression. She turned to face the Lady squarely.

"I can dream for my child. I can do dat."

The Lady nodded.

Tinkabelle, the Lady's light blue parakeet, chirped frantically and banged around in its bamboo cage, scattering seed hulls and gravel in excitement when the bell above the shop door tinkled, and a guest strolled in. The Lady announced, "*Kyawk-san!*" with a wink to Mama and bustled forward, a cloth drapery swinging out to cover the man who settled into the welcoming leather swivel chair. She looked as pleased as if she had caught him out of the passing crowd all by herself and showed him to us as her prize, his head above the white shroud now at the mercy of her razor, which she stropped meticulousy before she sprang to work. Tinkabelle worked at ringing her own little jingle bells with crazed screeches.

The bird never liked my effort to center on its nervous eyes. Staring brightly in through the cage, I tried hard to be friends with the skittish creature. Then feeling sorry, I let it rest. At least I had bangs to hide me when I needed some kind of protection.

For me the coziness of the shop became linked with the smell of sweet lavender-scented lotions, pungent astringents and medicinal creams. I think the Lady also sold cans of chewing tobacco and shoe polish, although I never saw them used there.

Once in a while she put me to work dusting off all the surfaces in her shop—they felt waxed and already smooth with age—and sweeping up the loose web of hair that customers left. I navigated around the spare sandbags she kept propped behind the door against the inevitable sewer overflow on a rainy day. The Lady showed me how to place equipment exactly where it was needed and work with vigor so as not to lose the least bit of energy or time. Each such motion flowed into the next naturally, because "Now you know da way to do 'em just right! You just rememba w'at you aiming for, *chibi-chan.* Yeah, den you go fo' it." When I did it well, she rewarded me with a grin and then, for Mama's ears, the familiar, "Plantation time, yo' Mama soo beautiful. Fo' real. J'like one dolly, Kyoto *ningyo*. *Honto ni*. Pretty pretty face. Dainty how she move. She stay shame so many boy like her." They enjoyed digging up the thought and laughing at it for memory's sake.

Their second favorite subject was old Filipino men.

"Eh, gotta watch out fo' da *bolo* knife. One poke! All *pau!*" was all they had to say, and we laughed until my sides hurt just looking at them.

Sometimes she shook out loose change from an iron piggy bank. Or she gave us odd packages of cookies or candies that she had bought from someone peddling. She wouldn't say no to anyone who came to her door.

When Mama and the Lady told bad jokes, they whispered to each other and hid their faces with magazines. I understood the kind about *puka puka pantsu* or "What did the cow *kau kau?*" but I had a hard time with the ladies from too loose and too long, which was something about France and underpants. I couldn't catch on when she made jokes about men who drank so much they went to the roof of the bar for free drinks.

"On da *hausu-nei?*" The Lady laughed until she had a short coughing fit.

When they got into discussions concerning strategy, they wiped their eyes with hankies at the recollection of past actions. Sometimes the customers tried as hard as I did to hear—I could tell from the surreptitious movements and stirrings—what secrets they were retelling.

Mama and the Lady called each other *yasashi*, sweet and tender-hearted, because they remembered the olden days when they were just girls with big dreams. Through the Lady's words I could see the younger face within the one that grew upon Mama. She had been pretty with rosebud lips, a little bit awkward, but alive with non-stop energy and so much desire for living. I learned how

Mama made extra money as a maid when she was going to nursing school. I heard how the Lady had a Japanese boyfriend from the camp who "neva came back from da War."

I wondered at those men, and the customers, too, and what Mama said about how some liked the Lady so much that they gave her extra money just to talk. None of them ever really talked, except for quick instructions, that I could tell. When they were done, when all the bald spots were totally hidden with carefully replaced hair, when they were dusted with talc and brushed off generously, when their tips were taken with a deep bow, the Lady would usher them out with a graceful movement and shout to their backs, "Come again, next time, thanks, yeah?" At most, they would mumble a quick thanks or gush a polite "Thank you very much" in return.

Once in a while the Lady would undrape towels from the face of a man sleeping peacefully in a swivel chair. She could handle several clients at once, shaving or creaming, cutting or expertly trimming, even massaging shoulders, each vacant body after the other, in a rhythmic order. She talked normally to us all along and kept her combs and scissors washed out one by one, at the ready for the next step. She moved fast, her body lithe in its starched white uniform and her laughter enthusiastic.

My favorite stories came out then. They told of the time they crossed over an ancient *heiau* on the Big Island, knowing it wasn't a good idea for women to be there. Although they didn't believe in Hawaiian superstitions, they insisted, the Lady was worried for some reason that she couldn't explain. Mama said they had already placed little bits of *ti* leaf in their bras and pants pockets "for protection, just in case" and thought they would just look inside the center of the rock pile to see what there was to see.

Set in a remote area, the place was totally empty, so no logical reason existed for them to be afraid of a bare field of rocks. They proceeded inward. But what happened once they were inside the compound, when they got nearer, was frightening. They began to feel tingling sensations on the soles of their feet, electric vibrations which they could feel even through their shoes and socks. Stopping dead in their steps, the girls studied each other's fearful faces. "Aiyah! What now?" They thought they were being burned by growing heat radiating upward from underground. Afraid now of everything they saw or touched, the two ran out, scrambled over rocks and never went back. Flies, that made them think of *obake* souls, covered almost every one of the rocks near the place they left. The very name of the place, which must be kept a secret even now, sent shivers through us.

They also told Pele stories, and stories about night marchers, as well as stories about blue balls of light, the terrible *hi-no-tama*, materializing above the graves in cemeteries. The best stories of all, though, were always about the two of them and people in their families, especially the men, who didn't quite believe in them or didn't support them the way they always helped each other.

I learned about a mama I had never known, one who was carefree and lighthearted. I heard about my grandma who scolded her endlessly, but admired the hard-headedness of her youngest child, anyway.

The lady once told me that Mama could dance the hula "j'like one pro," that she had a feeling for Hawaiian music and had learned from a real *kumu hula* in Kohala town. She knew how to move just right, "check her hands, l'dat, *polole* Hawaiian style 'as not so easy, you know?" But the Lady said this only when Mama was out of earshot, cooking our food.

There was someone in the background in the Lady's life, Mama explained to me when we had left, someone sick or dying over long years. It might have been her dead sister, the source of her real secret, which Mama made me promise not to tell even as she told our neighbor about the Lady's sister who caught TB. "An' den she could not get married, because everybody wen' know was gon' run in da family, neh?" Or was it that the Lady had to nurse her sick father who did not let her show her face to him? She had to put food by his closed door and leave, only to return for the dirty dishes.

The orchid plants, lacy in their full beauty, sat by her porcelain sinks, thriving in the shop's humid air. They, much like her, were not a bit regretful or secretive about their beauty. The biggest cattleya, a showy purple, white and gold, she once clipped off of its stalk for me to take to school, after she heard Mama complain that the teacher didn't even care that I was in her class. Over our squawked protests, she cut it neatly off and presented it to me with a waxed paper cone to hold the stem and her instructions.

"Look 'em in da eye an' smile. Fo' w'at stay shame?"

When we left the shop after sunset on our way back to King Street, we passed where a neon yellow sparkle gathered its biggest splash above a photo studio in a sunburst hightlighting the words, Sweet Leilani's. Men in uniforms of every armed force milled about there, waiting to have their photos taken with little brown gals to commemorate their participation in the recent wars. We had come from a place where the proprietor wore a uniform, too, though no neon circled the big glass window even while bright lights snaked their way everywhere around all the other signs of establishments down the row. We walked silently. I knew better than to look directly into the faces of the men hanging around.

But we rode the bus home proudly and smiled as people, one after another, noticed our prize. I protected that bright flower with my hand. Mama made a corsage out of it and stored it in our icebox.

On Monday I did as I had been advised, and got moved to the front of the classroom as a result. Feeling lighter, because my hair was now much shorter all around, I took my girlfriends' teasing, "Hey shorty, short stop!" as compliments. I also tried not to avert my eyes when the teacher asked a question, feeling for once that my answer stood a chance to be right, too.

When we went back to the Lady's shop the next time, I had made a colorful sketch of the orchid for her. She bowed to me in thanks, while Mama playfully forced my neck down lower to her in return as we laughed and laughed. Then the Lady handed my mother a tall orchid plant with a big hug.

"Fo' you, Kiyoko-san, da bes' one." She wiped her eyes in happiness to be able to give her friend something that pleased her.

"No-no-no," Mama's feeble protest didn't fool the Lady, who caught on right away when she saw how Mama gazed at the gift with her eyes teary, too.

During our walk home from the bus stop that time, Mama moved on fast ahead. Quiet, she was lost in dreamy thought. With me in tow and clutching her goods, she hurried to cross the street before the light turned. She held the flower pot in the crook of her arm with its spray of yellow butterfly flowers like a feathery plume waving above her head. Unlike the windfall she would bring home from the hospital, the leftover fruit or magazines or slightly wilted bouquets, these colors were a gift to her from her friend who knew who she really was. Mama's face composed, no expression showing, she lugged a shopping bag in her other arm. I could feel how she wasn't sad or grumpy this time when she swept into our street leading our procession forward.

*T*he second time it happened, she began to look closely at the neighbors when she saw them coming and going past the hedges. She had wanted to live in the area for so long, she couldn't believe any resident, anyone living such a good life in a neatly kept property, would do such a thing . . . the people in the old apartment, maybe, but not the ones in this solid neighborhood. The orderly row of mock orange grew so rapidly next to the rain forest which surrounded their green velvet yard, that she had stopped having the yardman trim it so carefully. She didn't care whether he chose to hack at the flourishing hedge which separated their lawn from

BANANAHEART

the undergrowth and the next-door people. The mock orange always filled out in no time, because it rained so much in this lush valley. She breathed in with pleasure each time she stood by the old-fashioned windows and watched the rain, which took on a refreshing quality in the soft light. No, she wouldn't let something so dumb force them into leaving.

Her husband, on the other hand, looked tireder and drank more, beginning each evening as soon as he entered the kitchen from the door which led up from the weathered garage. He arrived home so soon after work that she began to worry about how he managed to cut corners and race through the afterwork traffic just to appear, slightly ruffled and not at all curious, day after day, although his eyes always moved directly to the front door step. For Dave, the second time the bananaheart appeared did it.

Because the first time she alone saw it, squat and solid, on the cement flooring of the entry area, she thought nothing of it. It was purple and glossy. She had seen them before, on banana stalks, nothing unusual. *The heart . . . or maybe it should be called the flower. . .* Barbara pushed the dustmop across the room, over to the door where she studied it. It lay directly where one would step off the doormat onto the center of the concrete slab in the front entry. It was real. Their wooden door was screened off by an airy lath divider which gave them the required minimum of privacy.

Since their marriage and the move to the Nuuanu home, Barbara's sense of being the subject of gossip by those who watched her actions had almost disappeared. When she returned from the kitchen holding a sturdy broom, Barbara gave the heart or flower, whatever it was, a whack with the stiff bristles, and it flew out into the yard as quickly as if it had been blown by a gust of wind.

She suspected a dog or cat had dragged it up the steps. *Queer. But animals are like that,* she thought as she clicked the door shut.

The second mornng was a holiday and both of them were at home when Dave found it. He was reaching for the morning paper when he noticed it.

"Hey. What is this thing?" he called to Barbara. She was fascinated by the look he had when he examined it, holding it up for a full view. He dangled it for her inspection and smiled as if a child had played a silly joke on them. The morning newspaper casually tucked under his arm, he grabbed her and tried to make her giggle.

Barbara looked queasy. She felt uneasy. She looked around to see if someone were watching their movements. The feeling made her stiffen as Dave tried to persuade her to laugh. When he read her face, he became somber also.

In the bright morning light, the glossy purple skin looked almost black with shine. Faint red veins showed through the curl of the thick lip of the bananaheart.

"Dave, don't you bring that thing in. Probably has ants and you know centipedes always feed in banana patches. You can never tell what might be inside it."

They stared at the curve where the lip curled under. She explained how she had found the other one, then pointed it out in the grass, away from the entry, shriveled dark and gloss-less a few feet from where they stood.

"Someone's dog or cat must be bringing us these gross presents," Barbara said, hoping that Dave would agree.

He was silent as he continued to examine the curious spongy fiber, concentrating on the texture. He ran a finger on a crevice. He hesitated. About as big as a large man's fist, the pod was spongy to the touch and looked soft where he had prodded it.

Dave's mouth twisted. "What kind of crazy asshole would go around doing this kind of damn fool stuff?" They were both thinking of her former husband.

On the third and fourth mornings they kept watch. She stood by the front picture window, hidden by a web of curtain. He stayed in his easy chair positioned so that he could see directly outside by tilting his head just slightly. In his vision were the entry way, the yard and the hedge beyond. No one could get past the front gate without Dave's notice. He asked Barbara to run up to the steps so that he could practice watching. There was no humor in the request. She felt conspicuous, crouched beside the hedge waiting so long just to see if she could run past his unrelenting vision. She wondered whether the neighbors across the street were noting her behavior. As she tried to distract herself, the feeling of being watched washed over her again. She scrambled wildly toward the house. Barbara caught sight of the tiny pair of two shriveled hearts on the grass as she dashed up the steps. She gasped and silently returned to the front hedge. She had seen Dave's eyes on the other side of the window. This time she resolved to take up her stealth in earnest. He saw her easily on each run, however, and finally came outside to wave her in. He was confident that they could spot the culprit together.

"No way anybody's gonna get past us, honey."

On the third morning, they overslept by a few minutes and it was already next to the doormat. And on the fourth, Dave turned for just a few seconds to look at the clock on the counter, 6:03 a.m., when Barbara also turned to see what he was doing. Guiltily they knew what they would find again. The pile outside grew larger. They could not stop talking about the hearts and the only person they believed could have reason to harrass them by such actions.

"It would be him. He must be crazy by now," was the way Barbara saw it.

The only other possibility was the pet animal one, but the neighborhood was very quiet in that aspect. No dogs seemed to be walked here, and no cats or dogs roamed freely through the backyards as they had in the car stalls and lanes near the crowded old apartment. Since they had moved into the house, they had seen only an occasional animal.

They wondered to each other about the yardman who cleaned the neighborhood lawns. Could the old Filipino be slightly touched? There was no telling what somebody loony might do. Mrs. Wong next-door, however, swore that Felipe was normal and totally reliable.

"Numba one good worka. Always on da ball, and I never did catch him slack off. So wassamatta? You want me to talk to him for you folks?"

Barbara didn't want to explain about the strange hearts, thanking her too quickly and hanging up, afraid that the story would be told from house to house around the block if she said anything about it.

On the fifth day, while they waited for the heart to appear, Barbara heard a bold rattling sound from the back of their house. Something like a rolling tin can scraping along the path between the garage and the laundry area caught her ear.

"Watch the window. I'm checking the back." Her whisper wavered uncertainly.

When she returned, she was crying. "Horrible, horrible . . ."

The wash had been left out overnight, something she never would have done, except for this bananaheart business. She saw no one near the line when she stepped out the back door, but immediately noticed that some clothes were missing from the laundry she had so carefully hung out the day before. During that time she had felt watched again while she stood in the calm of midday looking upward at the billowy white clouds. She remembered standing in the sunlight trying her best to smooth out wrinkles in the wet wash.

"Dave, I'm so scared now. All gone . . . my bra and your BVDs . . . Honey, what is going to happen to us?" She shivered and moaned as she moved to him.

He embraced her, stroking her back in feeble misery. Sure enough, another one appeared during the minutes they stood together to comfort each other. Although he stayed home from work that day, they spoke very little, wandering around the empty house, looking out of the windows at the quiet residential area where all the other homes, quietly expensive and well-protected sat bathed in flat sunlight.

When the telephone rang, Barbara jumped. Dave answered the call.

"It's your mother. She said O-Baba-san had this dream about us."

Barbara spoke to her mother eagerly. She was caught in a stream repeating, "Yes, uh, yeah," as her husband began to pace nervously. He watched her face for clues. With the last, "Bye . . ." she turned to him smiling.

"Mama says it's simple. All we have to do is call the Prayer Lady, and she will help us "clear the house." That's what she called it. Mama already talked to Richard's auntie, and guess what? He's in San Francisco getting married to the chubby secretary who used to sub in his office. Come on, Dave, I heard the Prayer Lady took care of Osamu's wife when she got real depressed, and she was going to commit suicide. The family was so thankful. Don't you remember?"

"Barbara, I don't know what good it's gonna do. But you go ahead, if it makes you feel better." He stared at the front door.

"I know O-Baba-san always has those dreams that come true. Guess what? She dreamed that we were so happy, laughing and just enjoying life . . . she calls you Boy-san . . . without a single worry. That's what she told Mama today. Dave, we have to call the Prayer Lady."

Dave went outside to chuck the bananaheart on the pile. This one's purplish skin was fully veined with large red splotches which called the eye to the top of the pile of decomposing vegetation. Dave had not slept well for three nights in a row.

On the sixth day shortly after the sixth bananaheart materialized on the entry, the Prayer Lady stepped right over it and into the house. Her slippers, plainly business-like except for a red dot of fingernail polish in the middle of each instep, rested next to the dark pod.

Barbara was surprised. The lady looked so much like Mary Motooka's mother who had turned arrogantly rich from her dead husband's real estate deals. They were very similar in features and age, but Mary's mom drove a sable brown Mercedes 280 SL and disliked being reminded that she came from a ragtag, run-down plantation camp in Papa'ikou. So the resemblance was only that. Once she spoke, her gruff voice without pleasantries or preliminary softening comments, made them nervous.

She held her finger to her lips for attention and silence. The Prayer Lady reminded them that they were to tell no one what she did, not to insult her with money and not to ask questions about why she performed certain actions or how she did them.

"You had this property blessed?"

They shook their heads "no" together, both remembering how silently they had gotten married in court, signing the mortgage papers for the house in the same office. They listened to her questions about large boulders, palm or papaya trees, streams and potential burials on their lot.

"Under the house? What about *heiau* or anything like that?"

They did not have to answer. She read their blank faces.

With a fierce directness, the lady demanded that a bowl be brought out to the entry. She called loudly to Barbara.

"Yamada-san. Bring fancy kind, nice big one. Hurry up, please."

The lady reached into the bodice of her dark dress, an old lady figured cotton, and pulled out a book of matches and what looked like a tiny water bottle tied in a strip of *ti* leaf. For the first time, she allowed herself to be pleased when Dave silently followed her directions in placing the thick bananaheart into the large yellow ceramic bowl.

She threw in dried grass which she brought out of a cellophane packet in her roomy handbag, then poured in the contents of the bottle. She let the last drop fall; it looked thicker than water. An acrid smell rose from the bowl when she deliberately lowered a burning match into it.

The bright conflagration kept the three people transfixed until flaking ashes were all that was left. Only a fragile layer of blackness blistered the bottom of the container.

Deep in thought, each walked around the house into the backyard where the Prayer Lady stopped. She approached the cardinal points along the boundaries of the property. She asked again about boulders which might have been moved into the rear of the property where the jungle began. Satisfied at their ignorance, she shushed the couple. Staring into the labyrinth of growing things, she seemed to be talking to herself. When she returned to the neatly trimmed yard, she paced its expanse. One after another, she held on to the metal posts which supported the wash lines, then she turned her back on the couple.

A wild bird high in one of the trees chirped on and on nonstop. The incessant, although feeble, racket was unusual. Stranger was the lady's story about two brothers who were *tokoromon* to the Japanese people who once lived where the Yamadas were. The story seemed to have no connection to anything about the bananaheart. Barbara understood that *tokoromon* were people from the same area who were friends even in Hawai'i because of their association from the past. Only the last sentence of the lady's story made an impression on her.

Trancelike, the Prayer Lady rattled off the story as if she saw it playing out before her in the grass at her feet. She had turned her face so the couple couldn't see her expressions, but her voice traveled from high and young to gruff with an aged creakiness in turn. Quickly, she finished the digression, leaving no time for questions.

"After one brother died, the other went follow him. *Make*. No mo' *tokoromon*. Only the snake—long white snake—came out at night by the toilet. To visit the friends. To watch out for them. Only the children could see, but they came scared. No like go in there night time. You understand what I'm telling? They cannot understand the good luck part."

Barbara and Dave looked at each other, each willing the other to speak. They waited, instead, for the Lady to rise up from her squatting position.

From the rear her body was a surprise; it belonged to someone just middle-aged, while the Prayer Lady's features, once she faced them again were comfortably wrinkled. As they walked toward the entry and the front yard, David heard himself talking out loud. He asked her to bless their marriage. She did so. Very near the pile of what now looked like a heap of greying compost, the Prayer Lady gave them a long-winded blessing with her heatfilled hands on their heads, their shoulders, and finally whisking the fronts of their bodies from their throats downward. They registered some relief when she was finished; a tear crept out of one corner of Barbara's eye while Dave kept shaking the Lady's hand in farewell.

There was nothing on the front step the next morning.

In the midst of the big party, when they were finally able to enjoy the feast they had prepared for the house-warming the Prayer Lady recommended, they sat laughing together over the banana chiffon pies that Barbara's mother had brought for them. Surrounded by family and friends eating and drinking with serious pleasure, they had put the unasked-for gifts out of mind. Both were touched, however, to see O-Baba-san who walked slowly around by herself, cane in hand, admiring the well-tended lawn and all the plantings. The sexual appetite which had been waning in their preoccupation had come back to them as another unanticipated gift. Even their days now seemed somewhat simple again in contrast to the lack of order in everything that they began to call "Before" . . . once Dave made a comment about the past as "the time before the bananaheart blessing."

As they loaded plastic garbage bags with the party rubbish late at night when the guests were all gone, Barbara stopped her work abruptly. With the direct look which made him sure that she must have been watching him for a long time to find the moment to ask, she searched his face for an answer.

"You think we will ever get one again?" Dave caught the excitement building in her voice, and they both looked toward the closed front door.

I like to go to Long's on Monday. The sale is still on. Most of the things are still plentiful in stock, and no crowds make you wait in line or grab at the stacks of specials between people's carts.

When I pulled into the parking space, I felt lucky to get so near the store. Usually everything's filled from early in the a.m. I wouldn't have to push the cart so far, you see. So that would be a plus. As I dropped the keys in my purse, and I got ready to leave the car, I could hear the fighting. I got out halfway, confused.

Locating it, I saw the young couple sitting in the truck parked directly opposite me, sort of catty-corner. The kind of car all those young vroom-vroom boys own: fat wheels and a big fancy paint job. Must have been a surfer or construction worker. Japanese

A BIRTHDAY CARD AND WARM WISHES

boy. They were yelling back and forth, no way this and shet that. Once in a while, "Fock you!" All the loud F words coming from his voice. It made me go stiff. I get into a nervous stomach when I hear that angry edge in a voice.

She was hiding her face, making herself smaller. He was a heavyset one, his face like the moon, bright and crazy flat. He leaned over as if he might swat her or crush her with his hairy hand.

I said it out loud. What I was thinking.

"If you are abusing her, I'm calling the police." I was standing outside of my Toyota. My voice was shaky, but I said it loud enough so it took him by surprise.

Then he saw me.

"Get the fuck outa my life."

He swung his arm out at me once he got his door open as if to brush me out of his sight. He looked like if he had a gun I would be the first to be shot, then her, then maybe he'd turn it to his own head. That kind of twisted sick and sad look, but I got this electric feeling.

The others used to ask me to handle all the rowdies and the ones who were bad-mouths. I wasn't a school teacher for twenty-five years before my retirement for nothing. *Never raise your voice. Be firm and no nonsense. Take control.* I was a take-charge vice principal at the end.

"That did it. I'm calling the police." I said it clearly.

I walked slowly to the Hallmark Card place, the first store window, where I know they have a phone near the door. My leg bothers me once in a while. I hardly felt it, but I knew later on that I had been pushing it. Once inside I was out of breath and my heart hurt.

I could still hear him swearing to beat the band as if I were outside by the car again. He thought of me as a meddlesome woman, somebody he'd just as soon flush down a toilet as give the time of day to.

"Fock. Fock you." He said, "Faaaaak yooooo." He was screaming after me, having a tantrum and winding out of control.

We used to put the really bad boys into chicken coops— high off the ground on wooden legs—those boys got bug-eyed pressing against the chicken wire, their bodies scrunched up, looking so miserable and smelling like the droppings—when they fought and hurt each other or used bad language. Some benefits do rain down upon you after all when you work at a country school. They wouldn't allow it at all now, I'm sure, but it was a way. Half an hour alone did it.

Those days swearing meant a word like *damn.* Heaven help them if they said, "God damn!" Parents had to come to the office, begging us. Nowadays . . . people just turn away. There's so much ugly to see and wrong to hear that they just pretend they didn't and stay safe.

I could hear his truck roaring and screeching, actually lurching backwards then down the main ramp of the shopping center. The security guard came running, chasing after him, but it was too late as usual. You could hear the squeal for a long minute. How those fancy cars must take a beating.

My heart thumped inside. Too much excitement. I made my back straight.

Only the girl was left. She sat on the curb and cried into her hands. Just a child. She must have been a school girl playing hooky. But not, after all, a university girl. She didn't have the spark.

I was skinny just like that myself—but I had my teaching degree by then—when I married Mr. Matsuwaka.

He would have said, "Now don't look over there," under his voice, and I would have followed him closely.

He never liked to talk about why, just wanted me to follow his lead. I miss him now. He could have taken care of a bad egg like that in a minute. Matsuwaka believed, "Talk is cheap." He never said much for that reason.

He would have gone straight to the security guard at Long's and marched him out to where it was happening and never spent a second thought on was it the best way to do it. That boy would have only the guard to get mad at then.

My nerves made my fingers shaky dialing the telephone. Mr. Matsuwaka would have breezed right through those moments. Sometimes he treated me as a father, not as my husband.

When the 911 finally answered, I hung up because there didn't seem to be much cause for more they could have done. The security guard was already taking notes on the girl. Always wasteful anyway to duplicate, unless there's a need.

Sachiko came out of her back room, stood by me and looked me over. I told her about it and she agreed with me totally. Said how many of them cause trouble on a daily basis and how one of them threatened her—pounded his fists on her counter—on Valentine's Day, because a card he had wanted was sold. Said she was a bitch and other names.

"Those kids come out uncivilized. So crude and no class, at all." Sachiko was disgusted at that girl, too.

From where we stood next to the glass door, we watched her, still crying, for all to see. Big as life.

I remembered why I had it in my mind to stop at Hallmark's after Long's. A birthday card. Thought I might as well take my mind off the bad track and find the card now, not later. I didn't want to go out there and talk to that one, either. I might get suckered into feeling sorry for her, after all. Or she might say something vulgar.

Looking over the cards, I like to read what's inside, because it's shocking how many people don't bother. They just go for the pretty front picture. I remembered how Mr. Matsuwaka hated mushy cards. Myself I like a good selection, but my, they are getting expensive, like all things nowadays. Matsuwaka thought they were a waste and untruthful. But all I ever wanted was a handpicked one from him; it would have made all the difference— even if he didn't believe in the sweet words himself.

He wasn't what you would call a big man, but he made himself understood. He crossed his arms when he stood before someone and said what he had to say. He took joy in dealing with certain people, When he agreed with them, he shook their hand firmly and said a formal goodbye. Dignified. The rest he thought weren't worth wasting the time to get through to in talking, not even for a few minutes.

I used to worry at that whole thing about the talking—and words—why he distrusted words—never thinking that the time would come when the silence of his being dead would be so loud. My ears would begin to remember word for word what he used to say to me before.

"What do you want to talk all the time for? It just gets in the way of living."

"Why do you compare so much when you know that everything is different anyway?" Sometimes he'd pat my hand when he said that.

"Silence is golden." Then he would shut down totally. Read the newspaper neatly folded with his head and eyes straight ahead.

He parted his hair the same way every morning of his life, and he had the same thing to say to me each time I wanted to figure something out.

"Don't be such a discriminating woman, Hazel. Time to enjoy life." It was his way of thinking, you see.

I used to get so tired of hearing that. There were times I got so mad. The nerve. He just didn't want me to talk about something he already made his mind up about. Didn't want to share the why with me.

But it was his way of saying it that grated on me more . . . so sure that he was right, and I would never see the same light.

Emphasis on joy. "En*joy,* life, Hazel," as if I were some little kid who didn't know how to have fun. Wasn't very good with kids, himself. He always whole-cheesed the fun and acted like the boss of the game *Kodomo-no-Taisho!* Mr. Matsuwaka never learned to share.

But I knew that right from the beginning. So why grumble about it, except that he wasn't ever there when I needed him, and now that he's dead, he can't be helpful at all.

He was so happy when he was right. Overjoyed by his pleasure. He would call me from wherever I was, from my reading or my crocheting, and point out the TV picture or the newspaper to show me some official report with the news that stated he was correct in the first place; this guy was a crook or that state program was wasting money after all. Sometimes he said, "Right on the money!" or when he was right all along, "Ding dong . . . dinner bell!"

The best time for him was when he ate. He loved for me to cook. Mr. Matsuwaka—I hate to say this—could eat like a teenager. But he never looked fat, not one ounce stuck to him even when he cleaned his plate twice. I thought he would pick up like me after his retirement, but no, that fool had to have his cigarettes every day until they got him in the end.

Three hundred thousand dollars in hospital bills. I still get mad when I think how they couldn't fix that part in his throat, the larynx, had to be cut out, and how it still moved down so fast to his lungs and took over everywhere.

The insurance paid it all up, so I guess there's nothing for me to be chewing on there, but I can't help thinking he used to put those things in his mouth so that he didn't have to talk to people, and one thing led to another.

We could have gone on a cruise around the world for a few years for that kind of money. I could picture us on the deck of a big ship. We would be gazing out at the deep ocean and some green hills on far off islands. We could talk about that trip forever. But we were never meant to go.

He had a way of making me so mad. I got mad when he got sick and madder than in my whole life when I knew he was going to die. Of course, I was in grief, too. But he was much too young. The nerve of him leaving me just when we would have the time together to go on vacations and enjoy life. He was pretty thoughtless about feelings—so it fit. Consistent all the way.

I held up a beauty. It was one of those big ones that's for celebrating a fifty-year anniversary. The card had a golden sunset with glitter sprinkled in a splashy spray across the words, "Years of Faithful Tenderness, I Recall . . . "

But that's not what we had. We were more the cat-and-dog type of couple. Funny, somehow, how much we fought.

I picked out a birthday card from all the ones they had on display. Not too mushy or long-winded in the poem part. It had a picture of a forest on it with a red sky. Maybe it would have made him say, "Volcano weather," which is how he thought of a red sky, being from the Big Island. He always loved to look up at the mountains and this one cost only eighty-five cents. Not flashy at all, and it had the things he liked. I passed up the funny chimps with the jokes about looking older. Sometimes he would chuckle at the monkey being so human.

Sachiko looked at the card I brought to the register and knew.

"Oh, Matsuwaka-san, huh? You going *haka-mairi*. That's good. Visit the grave. Ho . . . one year went by fast, neh?"

"Yeah. I cannot forget him. In fact when my birthday comes around I buy one for me from him, because that's how we used to. Funny, yeah? I guess people would think I'm crazy."

"Main thing, communicate." She put the little package in my hand and gave me a big laugh. I knew she thought I was getting senile, but she always said that same thing to all the customers, so it was okay.

On my way to Long's I passed the girl standing by the entrance. I was not about to say anything—then I felt sorry—and thought—maybe, *Take care of yourself, now* or *Are you okay?* . . . When she recognized me, she gave me a look so hard, truly a vicious look, that I wanted to stop right there and grab her by the shoulders to shake some sense into her head. She didn't learn a thing. I just marched right into Long's and shrugged her off. Stupidity. All around me all the time.

Filling my cart, I didn't care what I needed from the list. I thought about how Mr. Matsuwaka would have done the same. As I did, not her. His cold fish eye was for everybody, you see, not just when he found a fool in front of him. With me he would clam up just to keep me talking, because I could see it got more interesting to him and he could disagree with something I said and then figure out how far he could change my way without words. But he never raised a hand to me once. He was never as angry as me. Or the girl. That wasn't Mr. Matsuwaka.

When I got to the checkout where they keep the flowers in plastic buckets full of water, I saw that the anthuriums were so fresh that they still had bits of excelsior and Big Island volcano ash—could have been dust—on their plastic wrappers. He would have spotted that right away. I went over the packages—even though they all look alike, some have tiny creases or spot flaws from handling—and picked out the best: six perfect anthuriums, the small ones, red like hearts packed into a tight line. Made me feel warm and bright.

When I got back outside, she was gone. I didn't feel relieved. I wondered where she disappeared to. When I got my purchases into the car, returned the cart, propped the flowers upright in their package so that they wouldn't get crushed and could have air, and then sat myself at the wheel, I began to cry.

It was the feelings that those kids threw into the air so freely. They didn't care at all who heard or felt what they did. I put my face directly into my hands and cried out loud.

No one could see or hear me, because no one knew or cared to be looking at the parked cars. I could only think about Mr. Matsuwaka when he was dying. They had him all wired, every machine was recording some part of him, every breath, every move. His chest was wrapped so heavily he could barely move. His eyes didn't notice anything; he was floating away by then. He always hated the hospital. The smells got to him.

He held on to my hand—his was thin and bony. He lost so much weight—so pitiful—and for a long moment he pressed my hand as hard as he could. Just like a repeated sound, a loud word, but I don't know what he was trying to say. I felt the bones of his fingers, those nubs pressing so hard and the fingernails that cut into me like sharp feelings exposing themselves.

*T*he you in there was Mama. This is what I thought when I saw her in the hospital bed, unable to speak.

You lie there as if you were already dead. Your eyes don't focus on mine. They don't open up big to let the irises take in my image. So far today the only sign you give that you recognize my presence comes just briefly with the slight pressure of your grip in mine. But the rest of you works along with the respirator, which is breathing for you, because you can't.

They did a tracheostomy to help you breathe. The emphysema is fairly widespread, the doctor said. He compared your trying to breathe to a person drowning, because the lungs no longer process the air.

YOU IN THERE

You have no voice. The deep resonance of your talking is in my imagination now, but I hear it as what I think you are thinking. You have shriveled. Always the biggest person in any room, the one who generated all the energy and noise and laughter in a given space, you suck on the air you take in and diminish in size by the hour.

The spooky feeling we used to laugh about when we visited this hospital remains in this place. Fears circle me. This is going to be your last room if you don't hurry to protest the way this feels. It's not like you to keep so still. You need me to bolster you, to talk you up and out of here. You need to connect to my energy. But first you must come back from wherever you are floating.

The soap opera on the overhead television screen is the last one that will play during your lunch, but you don't care to follow the plot that you have talked about for years. You don't watch or listen. You don't care what's on or who's in here with you.

Something about you now is out of focus. You look fuzzy at your edges. I hang on to your fingers, stroking the smooth hand, shaping the oval fingernails, hoping for some kind of response to my being here. I no longer notice the difference in the color of our hands side by side; what I care about is that you are not there in feeling, that the balance between our natures, your being so heavy and my being so light, is not reflected right in this place we occupy now.

The room where you are is pastel green mostly, with yellow and orange flowered vinyl wallpaper on only one wall, the one behind your head. Looks like they tried to erase the institutional look with that one bright touch. It's the kind of hospital room that you worked in for years, and the ward outside is warm and busy with soft-spoken nurses bustling around. If you would pay attention, you would enjoy talking with them the way you always question people about their work. The techniques are different, and they're using new, time-saving machines as they go around from patient to patient.

You don't care about the computerized thermometer the nurse tries to tell you she's going to put into your mouth. You don't say "Ahh . . ." or make any face at all. Your being passive is so unlike you that I look at you again.

But later when you seem to be more awake, you are nervous. You avoid looking at the doctor, the occasional nurses, the visitors who deposit flower arrangements, get well money, a *bento* plate on the bedside table. Your eyes don't stay on anything very long. You don't want to look at me.

Everyone who enters the room is prepared to do something for you. Everyone wants a response or some kind of sign from you. Some try to say upbeat, encouraging things to you. One old lady says, too loudly, "Bumbye come betta, *ki-yo tsukete!*" You would have said that heartily to any one of your friends before. You make no sign of hearing. The people who come in here go out carefully.

Your oldest living sister arrives before anyone else in the family. The nurses laugh about her later. "You rememba da one yesterday? She wen' ask at da section desk for Mrs. Duffland," they report to me confidentially.

"When she came inside hea, she look and look at your mother. She call her name, 'Kiyoko! Katie!', and then run outside, back to da duty nurses. She says, "It's not my sister!' J'like dat. Screaming at us. We had to go check da patient I.D. number, l'dat. She cannot believe her own eyes, and she's scolding us j'like we did something to yo' mother. Maybe we hiding her. Something else, yeah?"

Auntie Ritsi would be able to find something wrong with the hospital staff, that's her way. She's the one who always takes care of herself and keeps up with all the latest diets and health trends. She rarely goes out of her way to see you and always corrects your English. She speaks only standard English herself. It must have scared "the pee out of her"—your words—to see you so sick. Everybody calls Ritsi Minami the extra tight one. You used to call her Mrs. *Mina-Mina*, remember? Since a gift was placed on the counter by your glasses, a pair of fuzzy lavender stretch booties, she must have believed finally that it was her sister in there.

Lono and Ellen come in to see you and talk in whispers. Ellen places your crystal bead rosary in your hand and says she'll call the temple priest to pray for you. Lono strokes your forehead and says, "Auntie? Auntie, come home, okay? I like you get well and cook for me, all right?"

The other family members telephone each other, but it's the neighborhood who come to see you. They bring kids. One ties a red heart balloon to the foot of your electronic bed.

Betty brings you an orchid plant. "Too bad she cannot see good, yeah? Wait until she's better. *Kawai-sona.*" Betty blows her nose. Your eyes are open but not in focus.

The owner of the Arirang Bar hands me a bottle of homemade *kim ch'i* for when you get better.

They ask me who found you after your collapse.

One lady keeps asking, "Is that so? Really?"

Her husband says "Yeah?" to everything.

They are curious about details. They keep looking shocked.

They listen patiently to the story of how many times you had tried to quit smoking before they told you it was emphysema. I explain again how luckily Betty came over extra early with the morning newspaper and found you slumped over the kitchen table, how the ambulance took so long but was packed with all the equipment you needed to keep breathing once they got you onto the stretcher, how we were so relieved that you're okay even though you're not yourself yet. You look peaceful while we stare at your face and continue to talk about you softly.

The early evening is the best time for them to visit. The hospital corridors are filled and noisy with people who look for their patient's room. Except for family, nobody stays very long, though. Maybe it's the way the rooms are like dark cocoons with only a flicker of ongoing TV light, a slow motion aquarium illumination, and the flooring tile everywhere holding on to an undefinable, persistent smell. Or how bursts of sound from people talking seem to get very loud and animated then fade in quick spurts into all the other regular noises which flow on when the talkers decide to quiet themselves and whisper again.

Nobody minds when you don't recognize them. They greet each other, as if that were all they needed to maintain a pleasant, working face. The landlord of the next-door apartment building is surprised when you decide to smile at him. I am, too. We both try to talk with you, but you aren't really interested.

I talk about medication and therapy with your doctors. You would be very interested in what they say. They will get a psychiatrist to you, they promise, to encourage your will to fight. They warn me not to have false expectations as they talk above your blanketed form. Not even when Dr. Kaneshiro takes your pulse— you always judged doctors by how they did it—do you pay attention.

You don't care at all about anything like that. When we are alone, I talk and talk to you. You show no sign of hearing. You groan and make small ah ah sounds that frighten me, and then you subside into breathing.

You jerk suddenly as if in an animated dream, and the rosary falls to the floor breaking the string and scattering the shiny beads. Groping on my hands and knees, I search all over the floor and under the bed to find each one in order to string them up later. I pray for you with each bead I find. "Let her live. Let her live." I alternate it, out of breath but hopeful, with "Namandabutsu-Namandabutsu-Namandabutsu." I am too superstitious. It's not really an omen, I say to myself.

You stir and act alert, as if you are yourself again after an afternoon nap. I quickly take the opportunity. Because your eyes are yours again, I can talk to you.

"You can't just give up now, because only you remember O-Baban so well—maybe five or six people now living knew her at all—but no one as close as you, Mama, and if you go, all the true memories will go with you. All the important things about what she did and how she was will fade away from all of us." I add firmly, "You're not ready to join her yet," in answer to the thought I know you have just had when I mentioned your mother.

"And anyway, how do you know if there really is any life afterwards?" I go on, knowing I have you thinking.

Then you give me the sullen, mean-eye look. It's how you answer my comment. In that way, you remind me that you will have me remember that you do believe that dead people can communicate from that time after they pass on. I don't argue. I am so happy that you are yourself again.

I try for another run. What do I have to lose?

"O-Baban lived to 95. You are so young yet." You close your eyes.

I stand by the window and look down at the back of the hospital where an old wooden building is all that's left of the former hospital plant. I remember to remind you how long ago we once took O-Baban there to visit an old man who was dying in the care home wing.

"Funny, yeah, how when we got to him, he said he knew that we would be there before he died?" That story doesn't register for you. But it's the kind of story you loved to tell.

Outside, down there, the sunlight is intense and very different from the fluorescent light in the room. I tell you about how Baban liked to peer out of the windows of the old Kohala house to look at the garden. You nod. Or is it an uncontrolled quiver. No matter, I am so happy I am tempted to open the glass door to the small lanai outside to let in some real air.

But I should stick close to your bedside and hold your hand or wait for some word that you might want to write on the pad of paper waiting on the swivel table top. I am afraid you will write D-I-E again like the first time we tried to get you to communicate when they moved you in here.

I yelled, "No, no, no," to you, but you pretended not to hear me. You were sly in your denial. I took the pencil and put it away.

You are much better now, I tell you again. I should brush the false teeth in the plastic container marked with your name so that they will be ready to wear when you feel up to it. I should tell you encouraging things about how you will get better and be able to sit out on the little concrete lanai in the sunshine, just like being on the porch at home.

You don't talk with your body or your eyes. I don't talk. Like you, I make no sign when nurses come in and out to do things and make cheerful comments.

Your face has no expression no matter what is said, whoever says it. You take in liquids and food and medicine by gurgling tubes. The places on your arms and neck and side where tubes are inserted look like reddened, irritating entrances into your pain. The white-wrapped cut in the center of your neck is mysterious in the way its tube dangles, inactive.

I get afraid and squeeze your hand, hoping to find the safety of your telling me what you want me to do. And harder. I try to fix your attention on me, the most comfortable way to be with you. But you can't respond from where you are. Your hand wants only to pull away from any more pain, that's all. You drift in and out of sleep.

On the third day, you are up very early like a regular day. You look ready. You search my face, and I know what you are thinking.

"Now why is she here?"

I don't know why either.

When you die, you seem very relaxed at first. You have let me know with a hand squeeze that you understand me as I tell you that I love you so, and I want you to live. You tell me a clear No with your half-closed eyes and your shaking head. You ignore my anger. You sleep a while. Then you do open your eyes and slowly take me all in, and that does make me happy. But you crumple back inward by degrees, and I want you to rest. Your breathing sounds good.

An hour later I sit in your tiny bathroom preparing lots more of the Yes reasons. I practice how to say them:

You have to go on a "once in a lifetime trip"—your words—with me to Las Vegas and San Francisco and Tokyo, and you have to wear a big white orchid to my wedding, which will be someday very soon, and you have to stay alive to see your future grandchildren and you have to come home and sit on the porch and tell everybody what happened in the hospital . . . and you just have to. Because. That's the only way it can be.

When I go back to hold your hand, you are gone.

*M*y mother enjoys telling my young daughters scary stories about the plantation days. The girls always ask to hear about the Coffin Lady. Mama sits down by the kitchen table, her face busy thinking. Her childhood and O-Baban, her own mother, are ready to be called back. Mama pours us our sodas, passing out *mochi-*crunch or candy. Then she wipes her glasses, she has cataracts now, and clears her throat.

A long time ago, when O-Baban was still new in the camp, she used to be the midwife for Union Mill Camp, outside of Kapa'au town. O-Baban was young and pretty, yeah? But she had to do too much backache labor, because she was stuck with the housemaid work for Greenwoods and for the whole Sam Wells place, too. Also early in the morning she had to cook for all the single men down at Camp. Plus she had two or three kids, but I wasn't born yet.

GO TO HOME

She knew all the people living around there at the time, must have been 1890s, 1900. Those days Kohala was important like a small Hilo town. Union Mill was so dry and brown, though. Not like now. Not like when you folks went. In fact no more Union Mill now, right?

One family over there was not too lucky no matter how you look at it. When everybody was real poor, they were so poor people felt hurt even to look at them. Not just ricebag clothes like O-Baban them, this family's came *boro-boro* falling apart and too junk for rags. They were shame, too. What was the name? Kaneyama,

Tanegawa, Kurokawa? The lady was always sick, even from the day she got to Hawai'i. Ten years later on, when she already had four children, the *haole* doctor found out she had tuberculosis. Her husband was working that time as a stevedore at the docks in Honolulu, because Kohala-side had no cash money.

When she found out she was going to die, because those days there was no hope if you were poor and had T.B., she cried and cried. All the four children cried, too. All the camp ladies who heard about it cried and cried with her. Pitiful, you know. But they were careful not to touch her or her clothes or her kids. The others would move far away if she even coughed.

Quickly somebody wrote a letter to her husband for her, because the poor thing could not write at all, not English, not Japanese. And no telephone, right? The letter was in Japanese writing, but the neighbor's son tried out the English school lettering he was learning. So the outside of the envelope had on it, "Go to Home" in big, neat pencil letters. O-Baban took it to the plantation office. She always remembered those English words from looking so long at that message while she took care of sending it to Honolulu. She use to practice when we were small; wrote it in the dirt or the air, *Go to Home, Go to Home,* while she told all us about the lady dying.

The mother. So young to know that she would be gone soon. And she looked at the little faces, the children so young to lose the mother's love. They hugged each other tight and cried until they would have drowned in each other's tears. But O-Baban said to the missus, "You have to hold on, yeah? You have to be strong for the children until your man comes back." So O-Baban cried some more with them until she had to leave their shack. Later on she told us she would never forget how the lady looked: j'like a little girl herself, j'like somebody who got hit with a stick for no reason by nobody you could see. She was surprised and sorrowful, but she didn't want to let go of those children. No, they sat together holding onto hands, legs, arms, necks, so skinny—those days they had only can evaporated milk, you know. Nobody had vitamins, only rice, rice, rice—all one heap of sad, bony children and the small lady blowing her nose on one rag.

So they waited. But in those days the boat between the islands never did run on time, and anyway only four times a month, maybe. So it could be the mister missed a boat or never had the money right away or didn't get the letter in time or what. Nobody found out. He got back in time for her funeral.

The camp was taking it hard; yet plantation days people pulled together when the time came for whatever it was they needed to do. All the folks took care of the ceremony. The church people made the service just the right way, and the neighbors took care the kids, because no more outside family, right? They were all walking to the graveyard with the casket, just a plain wooden box, slowly moving under the hot sun. Nothing around but burned out, chopped down canefields, miles and miles of nothing. Was pretty near the old Kohala town temple, yeah, but they were so sad, all those people, because it was so unfortunate, that they had to take their time, step by step, remembering all the sorrow.

Well, the husband comes running up the steps of the temple and far away he sees the line of all those friends; everybody was there, and the coffin that they were dragging with ropes, and he faints. Right there. After all, he had to rush from the harbor at Kawaihae, jump in a jitney all the way to Union Mill and then down his house place. And when he saw nobody anywhere, empty, empty, all gone, he knew right away she was *make*-die-dead. All *pau*. He knew where to find the people. He knew where she would be.

He got up hard on wobbly legs. He rushed to the road towards the hateful box.

"Wait, wait, wait," he waved, yelled and screamed at uncle them til they all spotted him running from far down the dirt road, kicking up dust.

A big man. Strong, after all, he could do stevedore work, you know. Throwing huge boxes around. He could match the Kanaka boys, not like the other short Japanese fieldworkers, even the steady, hard workers. But that's how lots of those old men use to be those days. Try look at all the old photos Mrs. Hamada's house. The big box. Some were sumo wrestlers, giants. How they could find enough to eat, I don't know. Some other ones liked to do cowboy work, heavy labor and low, low pay. Paid in beef. You would never know how strong and big they use to be with muscles all over, when you see them old and hunching down. J'like the grandpas sitting around at Ala Moana Center nowadays. But those are just the sons. The first old ones were tough guys, hard-headed though. *Pakiki.* They had to be.

They saw him. His children came running back when they heard the commotion. But they didn't touch him. No, it was out of respect and fear. They stayed back, hanging around and watching up at his face. They were so sad to see him too late.

He gripped the box crying, choking up with sadness. And then he went force them to pry up the thing. He was one hard one, a mean big man, aching so bad that nobody would argue. They must have thought he was *pupule* already, anyway.

He was looking down at his wife's dead body. Now he cried. Tears were rolling off in two wet paths. And everyone who saw him felt pitiful and cried at the uselessness of the waste. *Poho.*

He talked to his woman. He kept saying, "I'm sorry. Forgive me. I didn't know. Couldn't get home. I'm too late." Over and over.

And then he reached for her cold body, so they had to try to pull him back while he pushed them off with the other arm. She was dressed so nice and neat. Pretty looking at the end.

"Give me a sign that you hear me, let me know you understand," he was shouting into her face, into her ear as if she could hear him. Her body was almost pulled out, because he had to struggle against all the neighbors holding on to him, begging him to stop.

That's when it happened. She gushed out blood. Her jaw fell slack open, and it spread out all over her face and the front of the man. Soft red-black. Everyone backed off. But he was satisfied. She heard him. Stopped the tears. He put her down carefully and said a prayer kneeling on the ground with his head against the coffin: trembling, moaning, coughing, but not angry, not bitter now.

Our O-Baban said everybody left that family alone for a long time after the burial. The oldest girl was in charge until they all grew up. They wen' *hanai* the baby brother with one Hawaiian family up in Waimea. Died already, but used to live in Makiki, long-time carpenter. That's the man who use to come see O-Baban when she was sick. He said he wanted her to guide him after she died, the way his mother would always come home to visit his father in dreams.

"Baba, are you going to watch us, too?" My girls exchange looks and delighted shivers. They each look away as if lost in a long-forgotten landscape, but they always remember to ask the question.

"Sure, I'm going to do that for you folks later on." My mother looks around at our faces, notices that we are all paying attention properly.

"I will always watch everything that you do. So that you will do the right thing. And I can show you how to come home when you get lost." She looks so tired now.

"What if we don't listen?" says the little one. She giggles.

"Then I will choke you." My mother doesn't smile.

There is a long silence for us all. I change the subject. But I watch her gentle face knowing she'll keep her promise.

We are very lucky.

*B*orn during World War II in a Territory of the United States, Marie Hara has witnessed Hawai'i welcome statehood and anticipate sovereignty. A writer, editor, and teacher, Marie Hara lives with her husband and two children in Honolulu. She is at work on an anthology of prose and poetry by mixed-race women writers titled, *Intersecting Circles.*

ABOUT THE AUTHOR

Photo by Kasumi Hara

ABOUT THE ARTIST

*J*inja Kim grew up in Seoul, Korea where she studied at E-wha University for a B.A. in painting. She continued graduate art studies at the Pratt Institute in the mid-1960s.

"Although I am always attracted to the Hawaiian setting, I wonder why I don't use it more. I guess I don't like to do the exotic, touristy thing. I don't believe in carved out claims—what one can do or should be doing—when it comes to art. I don't sit down and plan out my ideas, because I'm still in the process of defining what my art is. It's very elusive. Something pulls me. I just follow."

"Portrait of Three Sisters" 1991